THE ALPHA CLAIMS A MATE

BLUE MOON JUNCTION BOOK ONE

GEORGETTE ST. CLAIR

Thank you so much for buying The Alpha Claims a Mate! Sign up here for email updates from Georgette. I shifty-swear not to spam you. I send out emails once a month, with sexy shifter news, latest releases information, contest announcements, and freebies.

Visit my website:
http://www.georgettewrites.com

Visit my Facebook page:
www.facebook.com/georgettewrites

CHAPTER ONE

"Well, doesn't he just think he's all that and a bag of chips," Ginger Colby grumbled, watching Loch Armstrong, the sheriff of Blue Moon County, gyrating on the dance floor of the Hoot Owl Hoedown.

"Of course he does. Because he is all that and a bag of chips. And I'd like to eat his chips. Sloooowly. I'd lick the salt off them, and…" her room-mate and best friend Marigold picked up a french fry from her plate and swirled her tongue around it to demonstrate.

"Marigold, you hussy, stop molesting that French fry with your mouth. You'll give these guys ideas."

"I know," Marigold smiled wickedly, and sucked the French fry into her mouth.

There were a number of reasons why the sheriff annoyed Ginger, even though she had not yet been formally introduced to him.

The reasons were, in no particular order: he was ridiculously handsome and had muscles on top of his muscles, he had women dripping all over him, and he walked with the typical Alpha werewolf swagger that said "I can get any woman to fall into bed with me, any time, and leave her panting for more." The fact that it was true didn't make it any less irritating.

Oh, and the most annoying thing of all: he hadn't even glanced her way from the moment she'd walked into the bar.

Of course he hadn't. Why would the handsomest man in the county spare a second look at a fat half-breed werewolf?

As if she'd even be interested anyway. Her tastes ran to more refined men, she told herself firmly. Men like Ashmont Warburton, the very refined financial advisor who she'd left behind back in New York, who'd taken her to the opera and museum galas and who, unlike the sheriff, never strutted. He probably didn't even know how to strut. Of course, Ashmont had dated her for five years and then dumped her by text for a skinny blonde socialite, but the point was…that was her type. Except for the cheating and inability to commit.

She looked over at the sheriff again. The Gray wolves were the largest wolf species, and in human form, he towered over other men and other members of his pack. He had thick curly brown hair, tanned skin, and cheekbones that spoke of Native American heritage. He was slow-dancing with a slender, pretty bleached blonde with perfectly arched eyebrows and painted on size 2 jeans, and she was rubbing her body against him and staring up into his eyes.

When the song ended, he spun away from the blonde, bowed to her gallantly, and then walked away to the bar, pushing his way through the crowd. The blonde looked crestfallen and tried to follow him, but he didn't look back, and the crowd closed behind him, with clusters of women pushing and jostling to get close. The blonde stared for a minute, sour-faced, and then stalked off and grabbed the first man she saw, a tall lanky beanpole of a human, and they began dancing together to the sounds of Carrie Underwood.

The sheriff leaned up against the bar and ordered a drink. Ginger found herself openly staring. He was wearing a t shirt and blue jeans which perfectly molded to the muscular half-globes of each butt cheek. From behind, she could see the broad spread of his shoulders, and the swell of his rounded biceps.

The bartender put a tequila shot in front of him and another in front of the woman next to him, a beautiful brunette with carefully waved hair. Ginger watched with rising indignation as the sheriff poured salt onto the woman's neck and licked it off. The woman threw her head back in pure pleasure as the sheriff licked, and Ginger noticed that he took his sweet time about it, running his tongue slowly up the curve.

Man-whore, Ginger thought self-righteously.

Then the sheriff bit his wedge of lime and slammed his tequila shot, and the people crowded around him roared in approval.

"Caught you looking," Marigold said.

"Oh, whatever," Ginger said. "Just passing the time." She tore her gaze away and turning back to face her friend. Marigold looked like an elf, right down to the blonde pixie haircut streaked with black, an adorable, giggling little elf who always had mischief on her mind. It was part of the fun of hanging out with her.

Except on a night like tonight, when Ginger was still nursing the bruises on her heart and Marigold, as usual, was bouncing around like a bottle of soda that someone had just shaken, just looking for a way to stir things up.

Ginger wasn't quite ready to dip her foot back in the dating pool just yet. She'd agreed to go out to the Hoot Owl just to observe from afar, and also so she could tell her friends back in New York she'd been to a real live honky tonk. She, Marigold, and their new friend Winifred were sitting at a small table in the back of the room eating burgers and fries and drinking frosty mugs of beer.

So far what she'd seen wasn't that different than any bar in New York City – humans and shifters mingled happily, the music on the jukebox was modern and ran to songs like Zac Brown and The Band Perry, and everyone but her was having a great time.

She estimated that the crowd was about 60 percent human, 40 percent shifters of various species – mostly wolf, coyote, and panther. As a werewolf, she could tell by the smell, although the eyes gave it away too. Shifters had pupils that were shaped like the pupils of their animal species, and the colors of their irises came from a different color pallet than that of humans.

"You should totally do him, by the way," Marigold added, tossing a glance in the sheriff's direction.

Ginger choked on a French fry and coughed so hard she had to drink half her mug of beer before she could talk again. "Crazy woman say what?" she finally managed, blinking her watery eyes.

"Why not? The entire point of this vacation was for you to get over whats-his-dick," Marigold said, stuffing a handful of French fries into her mouth and chewing. "What better way to get over him than with a hot vacation fling? It'll be like a palate cleanser."

Where did all that food go? Ginger wondered idly, and not for the first time. Certainly not to Marigold's butt or thighs. She'd long suspected Marigold had a tiny black hole in her stomach which ported all calories to another dimension.

She took a deep breath and used her calm, even-toned, "reasoning with a crazy person" voice. "Okay, first of all, he has no interest in me. Look at all these skinny wenches rubbing themselves all over him. He can take his pick."

"Actually, I have been informed by locals that women of corpulance are considered to be more attractive in this community. And fuller figured werewolves are just about unheard of, so due to your rarity you would be looked upon as an exceptionally desirable mating partner," Winifred Hamilton said.

Winifred, an archeology student who was staying at the same boarding house as Ginger and Marigold, was studying the room with the fascination of an anthropologist in a remote Amazon village. She was in town with a group taking part in a fossil dig. Ginger and Marigold had dragged her out to the honky tonk with them that night so she wouldn't spend yet another evening poring over textbooks until her eyes crossed.

She was a pretty girl, probably, but she insisted on wearing her hair pinned up in a severely unflattering bun that she stabbed through with two pencils to hold it in place, and she wore oxford shirts buttoned up to her chin. Then again, looked at men with purely academic interest, so her lack of game didn't seem to bother her at all.

"I'm pretty sure what she's saying is, fat chicks are considered hot here," Marigold translated.

"Yes. That is what I just stated, although in a more scientifically accurate form," Winfired said, her eyes puzzled behind her oval gold-rimmed glasses.

"It's true," their waitress chimed in, leaning over to refill their pitcher of beer. "I would kill to have your figure."

"Really?" Ginger said, startled, glancing down at herself.

"Oh, my God yes. I'd be getting so much action."

Marigold had insisted that she wear a low cut yellow sundress which displayed the generous swell of her breasts, and which kind of made her look like she had a waistline by flaring out over her size 16 hips. She'd sprayed de-frizzing jell on her big mop of red curls and pinned her hair up with a flowery barrette. She had, indeed, been getting quite a few glances since she came in, and even some invitations to dance, but she'd begged off.

She'd chalked it up to the locals being polite, or the fact that as the new girl in town, she was a novelty. Although now that she thought about it, Marigold was also the new girl in town, and she'd literally gotten more attention from the local men than Marigold had gotten, which never happened in New York.

"So, about the affair that you're going to have with Mr. Hot Stuff..." Marigold nodded her head at the sheriff, who was back on the dance floor, dancing with yet another woman.

"Are you kidding me? I can't stand him, just on general principle! Look how arrogant he is!" Ginger shot him a disdainful look and turned her attention back to the big plate of salty French fries at their table.

"Why did you even want to come here, if you're going to deny yourself the pleasure of a mindless vacation fling with a big-muscled Neanderthal?'

"I came here to put as much physical distance as I could financially afford, between myself and that cheating, lying, useless pig of an ex-boyfriend of mine. Not that I'm bitter," Ginger said, and downed a third of a mug of beer in one gulp.

"No, not at all. I can see that."

Ginger's boyfriend had been considerate enough to dump her over the summer, which meant that she had a couple of weeks free before she had to teach summer school.

Unfortunately, on her grade school teacher's salary, she didn't have the money to go on a round the world trip or a swinging singles cruise. Instead, she'd settled for tagging along with her room-mate Marigold to Blue Moon County, Florida, where Marigold's 89-year-old aunt ran a boarding house. They were getting free room and board in exchange for doing chores.

"And if you like him so much, why don't you sleep him?" Ginger groused.

"Nahh, I'm going to have sex with the bartender. We've been fondling each other with our eyes all night." Marigold looked at the bartender and winked. He winked back. He was a muscular, handsome werewolf with big arms covered with colorful tattoos, a tight t-shirt and a gold ring in one ear.

What was really going to happen was that Marigold was going to flirt outrageously, then wimp out and flee without closing the deal, but Ginger didn't bother to correct her.

Marigold, unfortunately, was a love psychic. It was kind of like a curse. She would flirt with a guy, then peer into the future to see how their relationship would play out…and then it wasn't any fun to follow through with it. She also had the ability to predict the outcome for other people, which is what she did for a living in New York – but she refrained from doing it for her friends.

The music slowed, and suddenly Marigold nudged Ginger so hard that Ginger almost spilled her beer. The sheriff was standing at the bar again, but this time he was staring in the direction of Ginger, Winifred and Marigold.

A slow smile curled his lips. He set his drink down on the bar and wiped his hands on his jeans, and he began pushing his way through the crowd towards them.

Ginger's heartbeat sped up with alarm and she quickly dropped her gaze. What a player, she thought indignantly. He was going to come ask Marigold to dance with him after he'd just rubbed up against half the female population of Blue Moon Junction. If Marigold ended up going home with him, she'd end up just another notch on his leather belt.

Marigold deserved better than that. Sure, she came off as flighty and frivolous, but she was a fiercely loyal friend and deep down, her whole flirty femme fatale act was just a cover up for her insecurity.

Ginger half-watched him making his way through the crowd, while pretending not to look. He moved with a slow, rolling sensuality and perfect self-confidence, and people parted before him like waves in the wake of a mighty ocean liner. Women stared at him adoringly. Men watched with admiration and envy. As he reached their table, his gaze swept the women from head to toe, and a sensual, self-assured smile curled his lips. His eyes gleamed, and he glanced at Marigold, before his gaze slowly drifted to Ginger.

Unfortunately, his proximity had a strange physical effect on Ginger, one she'd never experienced before, even in the company of the best-looking of men. It was like someone had flipped on a switch to all the erogenous zones in her body and sent lightning bolts sizzling down her neural pathways. Also, her no-no parts tingled and went damp.

She squeezed her thighs together hard and tried to look away, but his golden-brown eyes were strangely hypnotic and she sat there staring at him helplessly, her heart pounding against her ribcage.

"Dance with me," he commanded, holding his hand out to her to help her from her seat.

What?

Dance with me? He'd actually just ordered her to dance with him? He'd come over to the corner of the room to graciously grant the chubby girl a pity dance, and he couldn't even ask, he just commanded? Of course he did, because what were the odds that a wall-flower like Ginger would ever say no?

Pretty damned good, as it turned out.

"Excuse me? No!" she spluttered.

Marigold choked on a French fry. Winifred turned to stare at her with avid interest. The waitress dropped her tray and half a dozen drinks crashed to the floor, but she made no move to pick them up, standing and staring at Ginger in astonishment.

Ginger suddenly realized that the music had paused and the entire bar was staring at her. It was like a scene out of a movie. And she had always loathed the spotlight.

The sheriff's jaw was hanging open and his eyes were wide with surprise.

"I'm sorry…what did you say?" he asked.

"Are you heard of hearing? I said…No!" she said indignantly. "No, I will not dance with you."

She quickly climbed to her feet, fished in her purse, and threw a twenty dollar bill on the table to cover their tab.

She pushed her way through the crowd, cheeks heating with embarrassment as Marigold and Winifred followed in her wake. Her original plan before she'd come to the bar was to drink enough beer that maybe, just maybe, she'd loosen up and flirt with a few guys, but that was going to be hard to do now that everybody in the bar was staring at her like she'd just grown a third boob.

Walking to the little table in the back of the bar had taken about a minute when they'd arrived earlier. Walking back out, now…that was an entirely different story. Decades passed and new presidents were elected as Ginger made her way through the crowd, who were mostly frozen in poses of complete astonishment.

Outside, bathed in the blinking neon red light of the Hoot Owl Hoedown sign, Winifred glanced at the bar behind them with interest. "That was fascinating. I feel that you may have unintentionally violated some type of implicit and yet unstated cultural mores in your rejection of the Alpha male's advances."

"You know, you keep talking like that, you're never going to get laid," Marigold said from behind them.

"I fail to see the connection between my speech patterns and the future possibility of my indulging in coitus," Winifred said. "Then again, I frequently have a difficult time comprehending and correctly processing the thought processes of the non-academic crowd."

"I think she just called you stupid, but I'm not actually smart enough to be sure," Ginger said. "Did I ruin things for you and the bartender?"

"I don't think it was meant to be," Marigold shrugged. "I looked into our future. It doesn't end well."

The night air was warm and humid, and a fat yellow moon hung overhead. Ginger could swear the man in the moon was glowering down at her with disapproval.

They walked across the parking lot towards the pickup truck which Marigold had borrowed from her great-aunt for their visit.

"You know, I think Winifred was right," Marigold added as they climbed into the truck. Did you see how the crowd stared at you when you said no? I mean, I'm only human, but I'm just wondering…is it a good idea to publicly insult the Alpha like that?"

"Publicly insult…oh, please, he publicly insulted me! Did you hear how patronizing he was when he asked me to dance?"

"Still. He's the Alpha, you're not."

"Hmmph. He needed to be taken down a peg or two," Ginger grumbled. "Besides, I'm sure it will all have blown over by tomorrow morning."

CHAPTER TWO

"Why is everyone staring at me?" Ginger said self-consciously, running her hands through her rumpled hair. "Do I have major bedhead?" She hadn't slept well at all; she'd tossed and turned all night, dreaming fitfully of the sheriff, imagining him running his hands over her body, his hot tongue tracing the curve of her neck...

Funny, in all the time she'd been with Ashmont, she'd never had a single sex dream about him.

Then she'd dragged herself out of bed at 6:00 a.m. because Marigold's great-aunt Imogen needed someone to help her gather eggs from the henhouse for breakfast and her handyman had recently quit.

Then she'd gone back upstairs to catch a quick nap while Imogen and Marigold made breakfast. She was not, by nature, a morning person.

When she went downstairs to join everyone for breakfast in the dining room, they all turned to stare at her as if she'd accidentally turned and was walking in on all fours.

"Is it true that you actually shot the sheriff down when he asked you to dance?" Miss Lamont, one of a pair of elderly twin spinsters who'd lived at the boarding house for forty years, asked Ginger. "In public? In front of everybody?"

"Yeah, I can't believe you did that," added Brenda, one of the archeology students, who all sat together with the professor at the end of the long dining room table. There were half a dozen of them, all girls. "I'd totally have danced with him."

"You'd dance with anybody," Tallulah, one of the other archeology students said snidely, earning a dirty look from Brenda. There was some odd kind of rivalry between the two of them; Ginger suspected it had to do with the handsome archeology professor Emerson Reese, who was leading the dig. He had wavy brown hair and wore glasses, and had kind of an Indiana Jones vibe going for him. He sat reading the morning paper, apparently oblivious to all the commotion around him.

"Everyone knows about it?" Ginger asked, sitting down at the table next to Tallulah, who scooted her chair over to make room. Tallulah was pretty in a washed-out, nerdy way, her hair scraped back into a French braid that she wound around the top of her head, her eyes made owlish by huge glasses with thick lenses. Brenda was her complete opposite, with stylish streaks in her flat-ironed hair, clothing by Hollister and a full face of makeup even at the breakfast table.

"Of course they do. It's the talk of the town," Imogen said cheerfully, setting down a steaming stack of pancakes at the table. She wore a floral a-line dress and her hair was styled in a white bouffant, courtesy of twice-weekly visits to the Kurl Up And Dye beauty salon.

"Eat up, dear! You'll need your strength to deal with this fiasco." Her eyes were sparkling with excitement.

"Who could have seen that coming? Oh, me. That's who," Marigold muttered into her eggs. Then she flashed a bright smile. "Who said that?"

Ginger felt a ripple of unease run over her. She used her

fork to spear a couple of pancakes, plopped them on to her plate, and poured a generous helping of syrup on them.

"How did word get around so fast?" she asked, shoveling a forkful of pancake into her mouth.

"Social experiments have determined that in smaller communities, this type of salacious news travels in a manner similar to a contagious virus," Winifred observed. "Only faster."

"Also it was in the gossip column of the Tattler this morning." Brenda waved a copy of the town's newspaper in the air cheerfully.

"What!" Ginger choked on her pancake. Damned small town busybodies!

She poured herself some coffee and hastily took a swig to wash down the pancake. "Uh…I'm sure this will blow right over, right?" she said, looking around the table anxiously.

"Sure thing," Reese said absent-mindedly, still reading his morning paper.

"Really?" Ginger asked hopefully.

He glanced up at her and shook his head. "Nope. Sorry, my dear. He's an Alpha. You're an out of town werewolf from another pack. You made him look like a fool in front of about a hundred people, many of them from his own pack. He'll never live it down."

Brenda nodded eagerly in agreement. He could have read the horoscope aloud and she would have nodded in agreement. Tallulah shot her a lot of contempt, and speared a sausage with a vicious stab of her fork, staring at Brenda coldly as she ate it with sharp little bites.

Reese turned to Brenda and smiled benevolently. "Would you be a dear and get me some more coffee?" he asked, holding up a half full cup.

Brenda and Tallulah both jumped to their feet. "He asked me," Brenda hissed, grabbing the cup and rushing off to the kitchen.

Ginger swallowed hard. Damn it. She'd made the news? So much for a relaxing, get-away-from-it-all vacation.

"How's the dig going?" she asked the professor, desperate to change the subject.

"Oh, can't complain, can't complain. We've made some excellent finds, and incited the ire of small-minded locals. The usual."

She hunched over her plate and attacked her pancakes, but before she could swallow another bite, her cell phone rang.

Puzzled, she fished in her pocket and pulled it out. Who would call her at this hour? Only her mother – but she had a special ring tone for her mother. It was the wedding march, which was a private joke between her and Marigold, because Ginger's mother had been trying to marry her off since at least kindergarten. Probably since birth. Ginger could picture her mother wheeling her around in her stroller, cooing at the mothers of other babies, "Ginger's single, you know."

The phone number was unfamiliar, but it had a New York area code.

Quickly, she stood up, pushed "talk", and moved away from the table. Could something have happened to her parents? It wasn't anyone from the school, it wasn't any of her friends, it wasn't Ashmont Cheating-Pig-lowlife-scum Warburton…

"Hello?" she said anxiously, as she opened the dining-room's side door and stepped outside into the yard. Marigold followed her out the door.

"What the hell do you think you're up to?" the furious voice of the Alpha of her pack crackled over the phone.

"Uhhh…good morning, Mr. Cruz," she said nervously. "Whatever are you talking about?"

But she had a sinking feeling she knew.

"Publicly insulting the Alpha of the pack? Is that what you

think is a good representation of the Red Wolves of the Upper East side?" he snarled.

"You mean when I turned him down to dance? Seriously?"

"Yes, seriously. The news travelled down here immediately and everyone is up in arms about it! You practically neutered their Alpha! This is not a small matter, Ginger."

Ginger's heart sank to the bottom of her stomach. Her father worked as an accountant for Mr. Cruz's public relations firm. Anything that she did had implications for her family, as well as for her entire pack. She just couldn't believe that saying "No" to some stuck up, admittedly sexy as hell jerk, would have affected her pack up North. If she'd known, she'd have danced with the jerk and then hightailed it on home.

"I'm sorry," she said, appalled. "Is it really that bad?"

"Is it really that bad?" Reynaldo Cruz echoed in horror. "Let me put it to you this way. Do you want to see me, as Alpha, challenged by the Alpha of Blue Moon Junction because one of my pack insulted him?"

"What?" Ginger gasped, stunned. That would be a disaster. No, actually it would be a bloody massacre. The red wolves were the smallest of the wolf species. Sheriff Armstrong was twice Reynaldo Cruz's size, and Cruz was a fuss-budgety, designer-suit wearing little city wolf. A Chihuahua shifter could probably kick his ass without much difficulty. In New York, the prestigious Alpha position tended to be held by those who excelled in business and social climbing. That clearly wasn't the case here in the more rural areas of the country.

"I'll apologize to him, for God's sake!" she spluttered. "This is being blown way out of proportion!"

Marigold was eavesdropping avidly, arms folded, with an "I told you so" look on her face.

Ginger glanced at the boarding house. The dining room

windows were open and everyone was leaning out, craning to hear.

"You'll do more than that," Mr. Cruz said icily. "When I asked him what we could possibly do to make up for your terribly inappropriate behavior, he said that he needs a new assistant because his assistant is out on maternity leave. I mentioned your particular talents to him, as well. You will be working for him for the next two weeks, and you will be VERY deferential. Do you understand? I do not want to hear any more complaints about you, or the implications for you and your family will be…unfortunate."

"What?" Ginger protested. "But I'm supposed to go back to the city next week! I can't stay here – they don't even have dryers! We have to hang our clothes out back on a clothes line! I ruined my best shoes stepping in a cow patty!"

"Consider yourself lucky there was such an easy solution," Mr. Cruz said, ignoring her protests.

"I'm supposed to be teaching summer school in two weeks!"

"That's been cancelled. And the renewal of your teaching contract will depend on your ability to repair relations between our two packs."

"Cancelled?" Ginger wailed. This couldn't be happening to her. She'd been counting on that money from the summer school job to pay off her credit card debt.

"The sheriff will come by shortly to pick you up at the boarding house, so I suggest you get ready and make yourself presentable. Good day."

Ginger stared in horror at the phone, listening to the dial tone.

"Wow. I will have to admit, I did not see that coming," Marigold's eyes were wide. "I thought we'd be ridden out of town on a rail, or tarred and feathered. But not that."

"How do you ride someone out of town on a rail, anyway?

It might be a better alternative. I mean, if I got to choose," Ginger said, mind reeling.

"I always assumed that it's like taking Amtrak. Probably a one way ticket."

Then, simultaneously, the wedding march ring tone sounded and the sheriff's patrol car appeared, steering round the bend, heading right towards the boarding house.

Sheriff Sexy-butt sure hadn't wasted any time in coming to rub her nose in it.

She heard the door to the dining room open, and the boarders trooped out onto the lawn, some of them still holding their coffee cups. This had to be the best entertainment in town, next to the drive in movie theater.

She quickly put her cell phone on silent. Her mother would, of course, have heard about Ginger's bad behavior and was now calling her up to have a long-distance conniption fit. Ginger didn't have time for a conversation with her no-doubt-hysterical mother at the moment; she was too busy panicking.

It suddenly occurred to her that she was still wearing her pajamas and slippers. Should she run inside and change?

Too late. He was already out of the car.

Mortified, she watched as the sheriff walked up the driveway and came around to the side of the house where she stood, cell phone in hand, future in doubt.

He looked her up and down with that perpetual quirk of amusement to his lips.

"Morning, Miss Colby," he said. "I understand you've volunteered to be my assistant for the next couple of weeks."

CHAPTER THREE

He smelled masculine and earthy, with a hint of some woodsy-scented cologne. His uniform was pressed crisp and clean, the tan polyester molding perfectly to the curves of his biceps. It was obscene how good he looked this early in the morning.

Her pink button-front pajamas were rumpled, and she hadn't combed out her big mop of red curls after she'd climbed out of the shower that morning. She was wearing bunny slippers. With button eyes and little ears. A gift from Marigold.

I am going to kill Marigold later, she thought irrationally. This is somehow all her fault.

"Absolutely," she said, pasting a big smile on her face. "The Red Wolf pack of the Upper East Side is happy to assist you in any way we can."

"You sure you know how to take orders?" He quirked an eyebrow at her skeptically. "Because I need someone who knows how to defer to authority."

Ouch. He wasn't going to make this easy on her.

"Your wish is my command," she said with forced cheer, her smile still pasted on.

"Is that so?" A slow, lazy grin quirked his lips, and she

found herself blushing. There was something about the way that he said it, the way he rolled the words around on his tongue, that made it sound like she'd just offered up some kind of sexual invitation and he was delighted to accept.

And she'd be darned if that pulsing hadn't started up again, directly between her legs. Throb, throb, throb. Down, girl! She mentally scolded her private parts.

As his gaze roved over her rumpled visage, she added quickly "I'm sorry, I wasn't expecting you. I'll go change. Would you like me to come meet you at the sheriff's office?"

"No, that'll be fine. I'll wait right here and enjoy some of Miss Imogen's fine coffee," he said, nodding at Imogen, who tittered and scampered off to fetch him some coffee. Damn the man, he could even set the hearts of elderly widows to thumping. He was ridiculous.

She ran upstairs, with Marigold following her, and quickly threw on a red dirndl skirt and white peasant shirt with red tulips embroidered on it. Then she stuck her feet into a pair of red espadrilles.

"What should a sheriff's assistant wear? Does this work?" she asked Marigold desperately.

"I gaze into a crystal ball for a living. Don't ask me."

Ginger quickly ran a brush through her hair, grabbed her purse, and rushed from her room.

"I've got extra condoms if you need them," Marigold added, following her down the hallway. "Do you want to tuck a few in your purse? How about a six pack? He looks like he's good for at least a few rounds."

"Shhhh! If he hears you, I will kill you! And are you crazy? I am being punished, not seduced!"

"Sometimes there's a very fine line between the two. If you're lucky," Marigold said with wink.

"She is lucky," Brenda said as she passed her and Tallulah on the stairway. "I'd assist him any day!"

"You'd assist anyone," Tallulah sneered. Brenda stuck her

nose in the air, sniffed "You're just jealous!" and stalked off.

"Jealous? He respects me too much to take advantage of me!" Tallulah hollered after her, fingering her gold purity ring.

She turned to Ginger. "He's just using Brenda for sex," she confided. "He doesn't respect her for her mind. Men prefer virgins, don't you think?"

"Errr…enjoy your dig today," Ginger said to her. "Hope you find lots of old bones."

The sheriff was drinking coffee in the parlor, looking out of place and yet perfectly at ease in a floral pattered wing back arm-chair. The house was decorated in early 20th century style, with faded rugs, china cabinets displaying old bric a brac, framed needle-point pictures, and lots of ceramic roosters. The girls from the archeology class were all hovering around the sheriff and giggling; they scattered when Ginger came into the room.

Ginger followed him silently out to his patrol car, where he held open the door for her and let her in, and they pulled away, heading towards town.

They drove in uncomfortable silence for several minutes until Ginger couldn't stand it any longer. He un-nerved her like nobody else ever had.

"Realistically, I know that you don't need me to be your assistant," she blurted. "You just need to save face after I turned you down at the dance last night. So how exactly do you want to do that? You want me to follow you around and act deferential? Like walk 10 paces behind you, or hang my head and act submissive or something? I just don't know how it's done out here."

"How it's done out here?" he echoed, looking baffled.

"I guess I don't know how anything's done out here. In New York, if I turned a guy down for a dance it wouldn't be a big deal. I had no idea that it would cause such a huge stir here."

"How about polite and respectful? You think you could

pull that off?" he sounded exasperated.

"Yes," she bit out evenly. "I'm pretty sure I can manage it."

He fell silent, and they kept driving. She wanted to ask him what her duties were, but she didn't seem to be able to speak without unintentionally needling him, so she kept her mouth shut.

Sitting so close to him was terribly disconcerting. He oozed sexuality even when he was doing nothing more than driving and staring at the road ahead of him; it was like he'd been dipped in a vat of pheromones. She didn't want to stare at him directly, so she pretended to look out the window while she watched him in the side mirror.

His upper lip was curved like a cupid's bow. The rational part of her brain knew that pretty much every attractive woman in Blue Moon County had sampled the sheriff's candy; the irrational part of her brain just wanted to trace that curve with her tongue.

The radio crackled to life. "Car 11, there's a Code 33 taking place at the Wishing Well Motel, repeat, Code Five at the Wishing Well," the dispatcher's voice said.

"I'm right around the corner, I'll take it. On my way, ETA one minute," he said, and activated the car's lights and siren.

"What's a Code 33?" she asked, as they quickly turned down a narrow side road.

"Burglary."

"Somebody's burglarizing the wishing well?"

"Happens more often than you'd think," he said. "And it pisses me off every time, because those coins go to the local food bank."

They turned down Wishing Well Road and raced towards a small, picturesque motel. The sheriff drove past the motel and up a small hill, where the well sat.

"Let me handle this."

As they pulled up in front of the wishing well, they saw a

skinny young man run past them, all elbows and knees poking out of holes in his clothes.

The sheriff quickly parked, and the young man dropped to his hands and knees. His clothes fell off him as he shifted into the form of a scrawny coyote. The sheriff leaped out of the car and followed suit, shifting into an enormous gray wolf and racing right out of his clothes to chase after the coyote.

He easily overtook him and the coyote fell to the ground, rolling onto his back and waving his paws in surrender. Less than a minute later, both men had shifted back and trotted over to where Ginger stood, holding out the sheriff's clothes which she'd scooped up off the ground.

She looked away, shielding her eyes. She'd gotten a brief glimpse of the sheriff's naked body, the solid muscles outlined in sharp relief, the massive muscles of his thighs, and the thick phallus that dangled between his legs, and she was struggling not to hyperventilate. Could she suddenly have developed asthma, at age 26? Where did they keep all the damned air around here, anyway?

"Good lord, woman, why you looking away? Haven't you ever seen anyone shift before?" the sheriff laughed, grabbing his uniform and quickly pulling his clothes back on.

"We don't generally run around naked in the city," Ginger said, looking away. "That's kind of a weekend thing, done out in the suburbs, and only with friends."

The young man shimmied into his dirty clothes. When Ginger looked at him, she saw he was just a teenager. He was wearing an old army jacket, despite the heat, and a grimy white tank top and jeans that were too big for him.

"Ginger, meet Cletus Arbuckle. Cletus, put back all the coins that you stole before I kick your ass."

Glowering, Cletus trudged over to the wishing well, emptied out his pockets, and threw all the coins back in.

"Poor bastard," Sheriff Armstrong said to her in a low voice. "His father died in a hunting accident, and his mama took it real hard. She used to work as a cleaning lady; now she's just a certified drunk. Doesn't do a lick of work. I may have to call in county services soon to take his younger brothers and sisters away."

Ginger winced. "Ouch. I hope that doesn't happen."

"Me too, but I don't have a lot of options. "

Cletus trudged over to Ginger and Loch, his head hanging down.

"God damn it, Cletus, you got to cut this shit out. Pardon my French," the sheriff said apologetically to Ginger, and she couldn't help but smile, there was something so country-chivalrous about the way he said it.

The sheriff turned back to Cletus. "You're lucky you're still a juvenile. When you turn 18, you're looking at doing some real time. Then who'll take care of your family?"

Cletus shrugged angrily.

"I told you before, if you need money, I can give you money." Sheriff Armstrong's voice softened.

"My daddy didn't raise me to take no charity," Cletus muttered, his eyes glittered with tears. Then he muttered something else in a barely audible voice, something that sounded suspiciously like "Fuck you."

"What did you just say?" The sheriff's shoulders raised up and his eyes blazed with anger.

Ginger cringed. He was about to cuff Cletus to the ground, and humiliate him further, or haul him in to jail, or…

"Hey!" she said brightly. "You didn't tell Cletus about the plan you were telling me about just a minute ago. Sir," she added hastily.

"Plan?" Sheriff Armstrong stared at her as if she'd lost her mind.

"You know! The plan you came up with! It was such a great plan! You said, if you caught Cletus stealing one more time, you were going to sentence him to work for the community center for six bucks an hour."

She'd pulled that from her memory; Imogen had been filling Marigold in on the town's latest news, and she'd told her that they were building a new community center. Her handy man had quit because they'd hired him to help put in a garden.

She turned towards Cletus, talking fast and praying that the sheriff didn't blow up right there. "Yep, he said that you'll have to hold down a full time job for the next…ah, two weeks, as punishment. 9 to five."

"I ain't afraid of work. Not like anybody would hire an Arbuckle in this town for any job, anyway." Cletus glanced at the sheriff, half fearful, half hopeful.

"Is that really what you said?" he asked him.

"Uhhh…of course. You aren't saying my lovely assistant's a liar, are you?" The sheriff was struggling to wipe the look of surprise off his face.

"No, sir, I ain't saying that. If that's what my sentence is, I guess I'll have to do it. When do I start?" he couldn't hide the eagerness in his voice.

"Tomorrow morning, nine a.m. sharp."

"Oh, and lunch is provided free," Ginger said, glancing at Cletus's bony frame.

He looked at her suspiciously. "You're not trying to give me no charity, are you?"

"No sir. Not at all," she said, noting his look of surprise when she called him "sir." "Everybody who's working on the community garden gets lunch free. It's standard."

"All right then." He nodded, then turned and jogged off down the road. Ginger waited until he was out of earshot before she turned to the sheriff.

"Okay. Let me have it," she winced. Please, don't eviscerate my Alpha, she thought desperately. I'm pretty sure my pack would ban me from not just the city but the state of New York. Forever.

CHAPTER FOUR

"Let you have what?" That amused grin was back, and Ginger found that, despite herself, a little shiver ran through her body and her nipples swelled into tight nubs. He was so annoyingly sexy when he smiled. "You're a puzzle, Miss Ginger. Maybe if I could figure out what you wanted, I could give it to you." There was a teasing quality to his voice, and a twinkle in his golden-brown eyes as he said it. As if he were picturing what he'd love to give to her.

Or maybe that was just Ginger's sex-starved imagination.

"Well….I thought you'd yell at me for what I did just now."

"Naah. You were surprisingly diplomatic about it."

Ginger winced at the "surprisingly" part, but she'd earned it.

"And that was actually pretty damn smart of you," Sheriff Armstrong continued. "I should have thought of that myself years ago. Every time I tried to offer Cletus and his family money, they say they don't take charity; I should have realized the solution was to find Cletus some kind of job. He's right that it's hard for him to find any work, the Arbuckle's have a bad reputation in town. Especially Cletus, he did time in juvie for a vandalism spree after his father died, smashed the windows on a bunch of businesses on Main Street, and a lot of folks in town hold that against him."

"I'll pay for his salary," Ginger said, relieved that this wasn't going to get her in even more trouble with her pack. "And his lunch." She could charge it to her credit card, skip lunch for the next few months when she was in New York…

"Don't be ridiculous, woman. I'll get the town to cover it out of petty cash. We do need that garden weeded and planted."

They climbed back in the car and headed into town. "Next time, consult me first," he added.

"Will do." She nodded, relief rolling over her. Disaster averted. Her Alpha, and her standing with the pack, were safe. For now.

"I'm going to take you to my office now, introduce you to everybody. We expanded our building recently. I've got boxes and boxes of filing that needs to be done."

"Great!" she forced a bright, cheery smile, but inwardly she quailed. How would everyone at the station react to the woman who'd publicly insulted their Alpha? And how had she managed to get herself into this mess?

Her phone vibrated in her purse, and she pulled it out and glanced at it.

"Boyfriend?" he said, glancing sideways at her.

Hmmm. Why was he asking?

"I don't have one of those," she said. "But I do have a mother who's apparently called me 11 times this morning."

"No boyfriend? Men in New York must not know a good thing when they see it."

"You're too kind. I had a boyfriend. We…wanted different things." That wasn't a lie. She wanted fidelity, more passion and a wedding ring, and he wanted to have sex with Bitsy Saperstein.

Her phone rang again.

"Why does your mother's ring tone sound like the wedding march?"

She shot him a dirty look, flipped open the phone, and her mother's shrill voice rang in her ear.

"What have you done? Did I raise you like this? How will we ever get you married now? Are our packs going to be at war?"

"Mother," she said, gritting her teeth together. "I am in the car with the sheriff. Everything is fine. Everything is going very well."

"Really?" her mother perked up. "Does he like you now? Is he single?"

"Mother."

"Maybe you could cook him dinner. Show him how domestic you are. I'm going to text you some recipes as soon as I hang up. Or maybe-"

"I'll call you tonight," she said hastily, and hung up. Loch was stifling a laugh. "Don't," she said crabbily. "Just don't."

The sheriff's building was a squat brick structure, with black shutters and a big sign out front that said Blue Moon County Sheriff's Office, with a picture of their logo, which was a wolf howling at the moon. It was located in downtown Blue Moon Junction, which was what passed for a town in those parts. They were gliding into Loch's parking space by the front door when the radio crackled again.

"Some kind of disturbance call at Terry Jones house," the dispatcher said. "She specifically asked for you to come, sheriff." There was an undertone of amusement in her voice.

The sheriff rolled his eyes. "Thanks," he muttered. "I'll take care of it."

He pulled out of the parking lot, looking annoyed.

About five minutes down the road, they pulled into a mobile home park. The homes were small but neat-looking, surrounded by well tended little yards.

The sheriff parked in front of a house towards the back of

the park, and as he and Ginger walked up the pathway to the mobile home on 3622 Sandhill Crane Court, he said to her "Brace yourself."

"For what?" she asked, puzzled.

"You'll see."

They walked up the white gravel path to an entrance which was flanked by artificial roses in plastic pots, and the sheriff rapped on the door with his knuckles. The door flew open, revealing…a voluptuous naked woman. Well, not totally naked. She was wearing a bikini made of saran wrap. It was quite evident that she waxed.

"Ready to unwrap me, Sheriff?" she purred.

Then her gaze lit on Ginger, and her face fell. "What's she doing here?" she pouted.

"Miss Jones. I have talked about this with you before. This is inappropriate, and a waste of county resources. You could have taken me away from a real emergency."

"But-" her lower lip stuck out.

"No buts. Next time you place a fake emergency call, you will be prosecuted."

Her eyes widened with anger and shock, and she slammed the door hard before letting out a stream of curses. He turned and walked down the walkway, with Ginger following behind him and struggling not to laugh as they climbed back into his car.

"Soooo…I'm going to go out on a limb and guess that at one point, you did hit that, and she wants an encore?" Ginger said, struggling and failing to keep a straight face.

"You're loving this, aren't you?" His tone was irritated and he stared at the road straight ahead, but Ginger thought she saw a little smile struggling to break free.

"A little bit. Yeah. This will make a great story to tell the friends back home."

"You in such a rush to leave us?"

"Oh, no, not at all," she said politely.

Hell yes, before I accidentally offend someone else and start a full on war, she thought. Or before I climb on the sheriff and start humping his leg.

Stupid annoyingly sexy sheriff.

He harrumphed, and turned on the radio, flipping through channels until he found a country song.

Her cell phone rang, and she saw that it was Marigold. She quickly hit the "talk" button.

"Oh my God, have you had sex with him yet?" Marigold said.

"Why, hello, Marigold. You know, he can actually hear you. I'm in the patrol car with him. He's like a foot away from me. So shut up, is what I'm trying to say."

"Oooohhh! Did he arrest you? Are you in handcuffs?"

Her face reddened. "No, I'm not in handcuffs. How would I answer the phone if I were in handcuffs?"

"Good point. Hey, sheriff hot stuff! When you guys do it, you should do it in the back seat of the patrol car!" Marigold yelled into the phone. "Or maybe on the hood!"

"I am going to murder you when I get home tonight!" Ginger hissed, and clicked the phone off quickly.

Blushing, she turned and shot a venomous look at the sheriff, who was stifling a snicker.

"You're loving this, aren't you?" she demanded.

"A little bit. Yeah. So, you're going to murder your friend tonight? Are you confessing in advance?"

"You hoping to put me in handcuffs?" She could have bitten her tongue off as soon as she said it. What happened to her promise to herself to be the only woman in Blue Moon County who did not stroke the over-inflated ego of Sheriff Loch Too-Sexy-For-His-Shirt Armstrong?

"Ginger Colby. I'd heard that big city girls were kinky, but I had no idea." His warm brown eyes were like melted chocolate, and a smile curved his lips.

Her cheeks flamed red, and a sudden image flashed

through her mind of herself handcuffed to her headboard while Sheriff Armstrong spread her legs open with his big, strong hands and... She pressed her legs together and shifted uncomfortably in her seat, praying she wasn't leaving a damp spot there. She'd die. She'd literally die of mortification.

She quickly changed the subject. "So, you and trailer park Terry – you never answered my question."

She was pleased to see that he looked uncomfortable. "Never on duty. That's all I'll say. And only once, with her."

"Never on duty? Ever? With anyone? In your whole career?" Ginger gave him the skeptical side-eye.

He spluttered and then made an abrupt turn at an intersection, swerving the car so hard that she banged into her door and clutched at her seatbelt.

"Cherry pie?" he said.

"I'm sorry, what?" Ginger gasped.

"You like cherry pie? We're going to Edna's house of pie right now. Their pie is excellent."

"Well...sure. Although I'm more of an apple pie girl myself."

"Good to know." They pulled up in front of a small diner style restaurant with a handpainted billboard sign that showed a perky 50s style waitress holding up a pie in one hand.

Ginger felt everyone's eyes on her as they walked through the door, and she blushed. One man in a booth let out a low, appreciative whistle as he checked Ginger out.

Loch's eyes blazed amber with fury and he spun to face the man. "Watch yourself." It came out in a growl, and the man quickly ducked his head, muttered "sorry", and pretended to be very interested in his menu.

The waitress lit up when they sat down at the table, simpering all over the sheriff. He grinned at her and winked, much to Ginger's annoyance, and the waitress nearly dropped her tray of plates.

Of course, there was no reason it should bother her. She and the sheriff weren't an item. They would never be an item.

The sheriff was sitting across from her, and she could feel his legs brushing against hers, and the physical contact almost made her whimper out loud.

She stared down at the menu.

Concentrate on the pie, she thought. Come on, Ginger, you can do this.

All she had to do was resist the sexiest man she'd ever laid eyes on for two weeks even though he kept throwing sexy innuendo her way,and also refrain from making snarky remarks born of sexual frustration, and she'd be able to go home in two weeks and put the sheriff out of her mind forever.

Piece of cake.

"So, those archeologists…are they still getting harassed by people from the panther nation?" Sheriff Armstrong asked.

Thank God, she thought. Normal conversation! Any more flirting and I'd crawl across the table and lick his neck. I am not a woman of willpower, damn it. My size sixteen ass is living proof of that.

"They'd mentioned it. What's that all about? They're not on panther territory, right?"

"No, but they're uncomfortably close. Probably not the best place for a dig. The panthers suspect them of secretly looking for tribal artifacts, and the site keeps getting sabotaged. Tires have been slashed on vehicles, tools keep getting stolen. They posted a security guard there, and the security guard quit the next day, said he saw panthers pacing around in the shadows all night long."

Blue Moon County was located on the border of The Panther Nation, a huge section of Florida forest and swampland that was inhabited only by a small, close-knit tribe of Native American shape shifters. It was strictly forbidden for anyone who didn't belong to the Panther Nation to venture on to the property unless invited by the panthers, and they had resolutely refused to allow any archeologists on their land.

Some of them interacted with the outside world, operating stores, bars, farm stands, and a casino on the edge of their territory; some were more reclusive and never left their land.

"Well, they'll be out of there in a few weeks, right?" Ginger said.

"If they last that long. I've got a bad feeling about it. I've been stepping up patrols, doing everything that I can to keep the peace out there." The sheriff frowned as he dug into his pie.

CHAPTER FIVE

Ginger stood next to a cabinet in the file room, putting away case files and pretending not to eavesdrop.

The sheriff was engaged in a heated argument with an attractive sheriff's deputy named Portia Sinclair. Portia was a reed thin woman with shining, waist length black hair, an adorable little turned up nose, and a sulky mouth.

Portia had glanced up at Ginger and the sheriff when they walked in the door, and stiffened in her seat. Another member of the sheriff's fan club, Ginger thought. And clearly she didn't like Ginger.

She couldn't hear what they were saying, but she was sure it involved her.

Well, eavesdropping was the town's national past-time, wasn't it? Time to join in.

She ducked behind a stack of boxes and partially shifted. The bones of her face shifted and stretched, her ears lengthened, and all of her senses, including her hearing, instantly grew sharper.

"-you have to throw them in my face like this all the time?" Portia's angry voice growled across the room.

"Portia, I never wanted you to join the sheriff's

department. You went over my head and got yourself hired after I asked you not to, so you don't get to complain that you don't like seeing me with other women. She's our guest, and I damn sure expect you to be civil to her, or I'll move you to the night shift at the North County substation."

Portia let out a low growl of anger, and then Ginger heard the sheriff's footsteps heading her way. She quickly shifted back to her human form.

What were they even talking about? Why would Portia feel threatened by her? Portia was beautiful. And Ginger was only here for two weeks.

She walked out of the room and nearly ran right into Loch. He stepped back with a grin, and she quickly folded her arms over her chest as her nipples sprang to attention.

"Everything going okay with the filing?" he asked.

"Absolutely! Is…is me being here causing you problems?"

"Not at all. I did have a couple of questions about your abilities. The ones your Alpha mentioned to me."

Ginger made a face, although she tried to stifle it. "Sure. Ask away."

"If it's something that you'd rather not talk about, I don't have a problem with that."

"No, no, not at all. That's not it. It's just another thing that makes me stand out, and not necessarily in a good way."

He looked at her quizzically.

"You know," she said, gesturing at herself. "This figure. The only werewolves who are, shall we say, fuller figured, are the ones who are half-breeds. So we're pretty rare. And then when I was little, before I could control my powers, I'd talk to people that only I could see. My mother had me tested and it turned out that I wasn't actually crazy, that I was communicating with the recently deceased, but people still look at you funny when you carry on one-sided conversations. It took me until I was in my teens to learn to shut it out unless I was actively seeking to speak to the dead. By that point, the nickname Crazy Ginger had spread among the pack, and it stuck."

Oh, crap. She'd just told him her very unsexy nickname.

But he was still smiling. No matter what she said, how dorky she sounded, he always looked at her like he wanted to spread whip cream on her and lick it off. Of course, he probably looked that way at every woman who was old enough to legally buy alcohol.

"Oooh, I think that's a wicked cool power. Excuse me for eavesdropping." A spiky haired girl with arms covered in tattoos walked up and stuck her hand out. Her fingernails sparkled with purple polish. "Hi, I'm Lola. I'm a secretary here. That's why I get to dress like a freak. So, are there, like, ghosts right here? In this room?" she shivered in happy anticipation.

"I do sense a presence."

"Really?" Lola squealed excitedly.

Ginger glanced at the sheriff, who nodded. "Go ahead. Let's see what you got."

When he said it, his gaze roved over her body, and she stifled a shiver. Why was it that everything he said felt like it was meant as a double entendre?

Ginger walked over to the far left corner of the room. The corner was empty, but she sensed that it hadn't always been.

She closed her eyes and relaxed, letting her defenses down, letting the world fall away from her.

She opened her eyes again.

"Eek," she said. There was a desk and a chair in the corner now, and there was a ghostly figure sitting in the chair, a sheriff's deputy who was slumped in the chair with what was left of his head thrown back. There was a gun lying on the floor at his feet.

The top of his head was blown off, and splattered all over his lap. Her stomach lurched.

"Suicide?" she said. "No, wait..."

His head reformed. He was sitting there with a handkerchief in his hand, polishing the outside of his gun, which was pointed right at his face. He was humming a happy little tune.

Then the gun went off, and the top of his head exploded.

She turned to look at Sheriff Armstrong in dismay.

"Was it a suicide?" The sexy smile was gone. He was staring at her with concern stamped on his handsome face.

"No. He was cleaning his gun with a handkerchief and the gun was pointed at his face. He didn't mean to kill himself," she said.

"Whew. Glad to hear it. It happened just last month. The coroner's inquest found that it was an accident, but there have always been questions. Poor ole Dumb Darryl," he added, shaking his head sadly.

"That was really his nickname?"

"He'd already shot himself in the foot, twice, drove the patrol car through a store window, and accidentally set his own house on fire. Nobody wanted to go on patrol with him. But his wife will be relieved to get the final word that it wasn't a suicide."

"That was so cool!" Lola's eyes were wide with admiration.

"Unless she's certified, it's not admissible as evidence," Portia snapped. She had gotten up from her desk and walked over to them.

"I am certified as a post-death communications facilitator," Ginger said.

"Got the paperwork to prove that?" Portia sneered.

The sheriff turned to Portia and fixed her with a cold gaze. "I just spoke to you about this."

"You can't reassign me. My aunt won't let you," Portia's eyes blazed with anger.

"Your aunt doesn't run this department. I do. Last chance, Portia. Now go sit down immediately." The sheriff's eyes turned amber, and Ginger shivered involuntarily. He was going all Alpha on Portia, and he was a damned scary sight when he did that.

Portia turned stiffly and walked back to her desk.

"Forget about her," Lola whispered.

Ginger winced. She had a feeling it wouldn't be that easy.

As she walked back to the filing room, she saw another werewolf watching her with a frown. He was a handsome, broad-shouldered man who was almost as muscular as Sheriff Armstrong. Loch walked over to her and introduced her to him.

"Ginger, this is Jax Mackenzie, my lieutenant. Jax, this is our special guest. You've heard all about her."

"Sure did." He flashed a brief smile at that, and Ginger almost snickered, but sobered up quickly as she remembered how much trouble her little gaffe had caused. "Pleased to meet you," she said, and he nodded at her with no expression on his face, and went back to the case file he'd been studying.

"He doesn't like me, does he?" Ginger asked in a low voice as the sheriff walked back to the file room with her.

"He doesn't like anybody. Don't take it personally."

Ginger forced a smile, and glanced back at Portia, who was staring at her with eyes like daggers. When Portia saw her looking, she scowled and her gaze immediately dropped to her desk.

It's going to be a long damned two weeks, Ginger thought, stepping into the file room and shutting the door firmly behind her.

CHAPTER SIX

"Marigold, you've got a visitor. And a handsome one, at that."
Imogen's creaky voice drifted into the sitting room, where
Marigold, Ginger, and most of the half dozen students from
the archeology group were playing spades.

Brenda and the professor were nowhere in sight. Tallulah's
gaze kept snapping up every time they heard a noise in the
hallway, and then when the professor failed to reappear, her
face would fall and she'd turn back to the card game.

They all looked up as the bartender from the Hoot Owl
walked into the room. He wore jeans and motorcycle boots
and a t-shirt with a skull on it. If Ginger wasn't trying to find
off unwanted erotic thoughts about the sheriff, she'd have
found him totally hot.

"Hey, can I talk to you outside for a minute?" he asked
Marigold.

"Uhh…" she glanced at Ginger, startled.

"Yes, she can!" Ginger called out.

Marigold shot her an "I know where you sleep" look,
stood up, and gestured at Ginger to come with her. They
walked outside, standing in front of the boarding house.

A warm wind ruffled the branches of the trees, and a

chorus of crickets creaked in the background. The stars were like hard bright diamonds set in a cloudless, black velvet sky. Ginger couldn't remember the last time she'd looked at the sky when she was in the city.

"You left before I got a chance to ask you out last night," the bartender said. "My name's Henry, by the way."

He stuck out his hand and Marigold shook it.

"Sorry, I ah…"

"It's my fault she left. That whole thing with the sheriff," Ginger said. "The temperature in the room suddenly dropped 50 degrees and it seemed safest to head for the hills."

"Oh yeah." He chuckled. "That was classic. I don't think a woman's ever turned him down before. It was beautiful." Then his face grew serious. "Don't tell him I said that. Please. Seriously. Don't."

"I won't," Ginger promised.

He turned to Marigold. "So – dinner tomorrow night? I could pick you up around six?"

"Uhh, well – the thing is-"

"The thing is, she'd love to!" Ginger jumped in.

"Great!" Henry's face lit up in a smile. Then he stood there awkwardly for a minute while Margiold flashed a pained, polite smile. "Well, I don't want to keep you. I'll let you get back to your card game."

Marigold waited until he left to turn on Ginger with a scowl. "What the heck? There's a reason I left without talking to him last night. I already looked into our future. I saw me going back to New York by myself. And crying."

"You know what? You really need to stop looking into your own love future. It's ruining your love life."

"Or saving it," Marigold grumbled. "Wouldn't you have wanted to know what was going to happen with Sir Douche A Lot, back in New York?"

"I don't know. Not necessarily. Yeah, it sucked, but you can't live your whole life in fear of making a mistake. Maybe you need to have the life experiences that you're meant to have, even the bad ones, so you can become the person that you're meant to be."

"What? That was so convoluted, you almost sounded like Winifred just now. Could you please make sense?"

"Just freaking go out on a date with him. Just this one date, and then I won't nag you any more."

"Fine. If you go out on a date with Sheriff Sexy Ass, I will go out on a date with Henry."

"He hasn't asked me," Ginger said. "And he's not going to." She was pretty sure, anyway. For all his flirting, at the end of the day, he'd just dropped her off at the boarding house with a wink and a good night wave.

She had a feeling he flirted as a natural reflex, like breathing.

"Yes, he will. And no, I didn't look into your future, I can just tell. Promise me that when he asks you out, not if, you will say yes. And I'll go out on a date with Henry."

"All right then, I will," Ginger said. Ha. That was an easy promise. The sheriff would ask her out when pigs fly.

Ginger woke up early the next morning so she'd have time to shower, get dressed, and be ready when the sheriff came for her at 8. No way was he catching her in her pajamas again.

She tried on half a dozen outfits, finally settling on a pink shirt and pink floral skirt.

Staring in the mirror, she tugged at the neckline of her scoop neck shirt. Too much cleavage? Too little? One of the advantages of being a larger woman was having big breasts. Then again, she didn't want to look like a floozy. She yanked the neckline back up.

Did the sheriff like big breasts? She wondered. Not that it mattered, of course.

Ashmont had not been fond of any display of her cleavage. He was easily embarrassed, and before he took her out anywhere he'd spend half an hour fussing at her clothes, yanking them around, readjusting them, picking out different accessories for her.

At the time, she'd told herself that she was lucky she'd found a straight man who actually cared about fashion.

Now that they'd split up she had to admit to herself that his fashion advice was always laced with subtle insults. He was constantly telling her to dress to hide her figure. "Wear this sash to make it look like you've got a waistline," he'd say.

"Of course he'll choose me. Ever heard of the Madonna Whore complex? Men have sex with sluts, but they marry virgins," Tallulah's smug voice drifted down the hall.

Ginger groaned and wished there was another way down to the dining room. She shut her door behind her, rounded the corner and walked down the stairs, where Tallulah and Brenda were standing locked in a heated argument. They both swung around as she walked towards them.

"Who do you think a man would want to marry? Some loose-coochie hoebag or a virtuous soul-mate who's saving herself for marriage?" Tallulah demanded.

"Bitch, what did you call me?" Rage flared on Brenda's face and she gave Tallulah a hard shove. Tallulah let out a shriek and stumbled backwards, and Ginger barely had time to grab her before she fell.

"You're not just a skank, you're a crazy skank! I'm telling Professor Reese!" Tallulah screamed, hiding behind Ginger as Ginger quickly herded her down the stairs.

"Go ahead! I'll tell him what you called me!" Brenda yelled back.

"He already knows about your loose coochie, you slut!"

Ginger stopped and threw her arms out between the two of them and yelled, in her best school-marm voice, "Stop it immediately and act your age or there will be consequences!"

They both settled down, shooting each other venomous glares and muttering under their breath.

"Both of you are risking getting thrown out of school, do

you realize that? And if anyone thought that Professor Reese was romantically involved with any of his students, which I'm sure he's not, he could be suspended from the university. Or fired. Is that what you want?'

Both of them hung their heads and muttered sullen "No's" as they marched into the dining room. Professor Reese was already there, digging into a cheese omelet.

"So, how is our newest sheriff's deputy?" Professor Reese asked cheerfully, as Tallulah took a seat on one side of him and Brenda sat down on the other side. He seemed completely unaware of all the tension that he was causing.

Winifred watched both of them with a quizzical expression on her face. Ginger imagined that she was probably composing a thesis proposal based on their behavior.

"Fine, thank you."

"Pass me the butter, will you, my dear?" said the professor. The butter was a foot away from him, Ginger thought with exasperation, but she reached for it. "I'll do it!" Tallulah said hastily, and leaped up, reached over the table, grabbed the butter, and set it in front him.

"Thank you, angel." He beamed at her approvingly, and Brenda rolled her eyes and made a gagging motion.

Tallulah practically glowed at the compliment.

"By the way, you look very nice. I see you've finally started taking my advice and you're putting on some makeup. Just in time for your ridealong," Marigold said smugly. "I look forward to hearing all the details of your hot date."

"How many times do I have to tell you, he doesn't like me in that way? And the feeling's mutual. He's bossy and smug."

"If he didn't like you in that way, he wouldn't have you riding along in his car with him all day long; he'd stick you in the office doing paperwork and answering phones. As for his personality, when he was waiting for you to get ready yesterday he was absolutely charming. I think you're the one with personality issues."

"You know, a lapful of hot coffee would severely cramp your style with the local boys," Ginger said threateningly, nudging her mug with her elbow. "It would leave blisters."

"I ain't a-scaired of you," Marigold said, but she scooted her chair away so she was out of Ginger's reach.

"So are things going well on the dig?" Ginger asked the professor. "The sheriff mentioned that the Panther Nation have been giving you some grief."

"Unfortunately, that's true," the professor nodded. "But we're not going to let them scare us off. Are we, girls?" He beamed at his students.

They all shook their heads fervently, staring at him with adoring eyes.

"Why do they think that you're after their artifacts?"

"Oh, just paranoia and suspicion of outsiders." He waved his hand dismissively. "They're trying to claim we're here to steal their tribal artifacts, but we're not. We're working a very promising fossil bed from the paleolithic area. We've found mastodon bones and teeth. We've very clearly demonstrated the legitimacy of our dig." He shrugged, as if he didn't have a care in the world.

The floorboards creaked as the new handyman walked in. Ginger saw Marigold's eyes flick appreciatively at him. He was a good looking specimen. A panther shifter, he was muscular and had long black hair tied back in a ponytail, and he wore tight jeans and a tank top. He carried a tool box with him.

"Everything okay in here, folks?" he asked. "I just need to measure these windows so I can put in new frames, if it's not a bother."

"That is a fascinating regional dialect," Winifred said. "Is your original pack domicile located in regions Northwest of here?"

"Uhhhh…." He stared at her, baffled.

"She's saying she loves your accent and asking where you from," Marigold jumped in helpfully.

"Oh! Thank you, ma'am. My folks hail from Alabama," he nodded politely and walked to the end of the room with his toolbox. Winifred's gaze briefly followed him and then she quickly turned back to her plate of eggs. Ginger thought that Winifred

A car horn blared out front, making Ginger jump.

"Lover boy's here!" Marigold trilled.

"Watch yourself, or I swear I'll…I swear I'll…"

"You'll what?"

"I'll make empty threats of violent retribution which I have no intention of actually carrying out," Ginger snapped.

"Yeah, I thought so. Enjoy. Especially when he asks you out on a date. And you're not allowed to say no because you promised," Marigold said smugly.

When she got outside, the sheriff was standing outside the cruiser holding her door open for her. Ginger grudgingly had to admit that, even if the sheriff was the biggest flirt in Blue Moon County, at least he was a gentleman. She tried to remember if Ashmont had ever opened doors for her. Ashmont was big on women's lib, which was usually nice, but every once in a while, a woman just wants to be treated like a lady, Ginger thought.

"You look nice today," Loch said, giving her an appreciative once-over.

Ginger blushed. "Why, thank you," she said. "Just something I threw on." After half a dozen outfit changes. "What's on the agenda for today?"

"This morning we'll just cruise around town for a little while. I thought you might like to go for a run later. I could show you some of the sights."

"A run? In the woods?" Ginger asked, startled.

He gave her that smile again, the slow, amused curl of his lips that made her heart beat faster and heat pool between her legs. That smile should be registered as a lethal weapon, she thought. It was just unfair.

"That's where we usually do it out here. We can run through the center of town, if you want."

"You mean, like, a run…without our clothes on?" a blush crept over her cheek and up her throat.

"Well, darlin', I've never shifted and run in my clothes. Have you?"

"Er, no. But I'm a little self conscious about my body," she muttered. A little? A little didn't even begin to cover it.

He glanced at her, his gaze running slowly up and down her body like a warm caress, and she quickly crossed her arms over her chest to cover the hardening of her nipples.

"Why? You're blessed, the way I see it."

She'd never seen it as a blessing. The constant stares and questions had started in kindergarten and had never let up. "My, you're quite…unusual looking for a werewolf."

She had to admit, though, the appreciative stares she'd gotten from men ever since she'd arrived in Blue Moon Junction were quite gratifying.

Before he could pursue the topic of going for a run any more, his cell phone jangled in his pocket and he pulled it out.

"Hello, grandmother. Right now? You sure you need my help right now? Maybe I could send over one of the boys instead? All right, fine, I'll come over."

He sighed. "We're taking a brief detour over to my grandmother's house. Hope you don't mind."

"Of course not," she said with a smile. Especially because, if his family was anything like hers, there was major potential for watching his grandmother embarrass the heck out of him. Ginger was supposed to behave herself around the sheriff, but that didn't mean that she couldn't live vicariously.

His grandmother lived on the outskirts of town, in an old red farmhouse with an iron rooster weathervane on the roof.

She was waiting for them on the front porch when they pulled up. She waved at them as they walked up her driveway, beaming at Ginger. She was short and chubby and her hair was piled high in a bun on top of her head.

"Well, hello, hello!" she smiled, and held out her hand to shake Ginger's hand. "I'm Wilhelmina, but my friends call me Willie. Do come in, I've made iced tea."

"I thought you said the fence needed mending." The sheriff shot a narrow-eyed look at his grandmother. "You said all the horses were going to get out and run into the road."

"Oh, it was just one fence post was leaning over a little bit. I pushed it back up. Iced tea's on the kitchen table. Don't be rude to your guest, now."

"Grandmother...." Loch said, shooting his grandmother an indignant look as they trooped inside.

"Yes? By the way, she's every bit as pretty as everybody's been saying." Willie's voice sank to a whisper. "She's got childbearing hips. I approve."

"Grandmother! Seriously! I will turn around and leave right now."

Ginger was delighted to see a stain of red on those broad, high cheekbones. The sheriff was actually blushing.

The sheriff, usually so self-assured and in control, was utterly mortified by his grandmother, and there was not a thing he could do about it.

The kitchen was decorated with pictures of wolves of all ages. There was a long wooden table in the center of the room. Willie had set out sweet tea in mason jars topped with sprigs of mint, along with plates piled high with meltingly sweet chocolate brownies.

"This tea is delicious. I've never tasted anything like it," Ginger said.

"Ancient family recipe. Of course, if you were going to settle down here, I'd share it with you."

"You'll have to excuse my grandmother," the sheriff said, shooting Wilhelmina a warning look, which she ignored as she poured more tea for Ginger. "She's becoming extremely senile."

"Nonsense. How are your brownies, dear?"

"Incredibly delicious," Ginger grinned. This trip had turned out to be an unexpected treat. The sheriff had been making her squirm for days now; it was fun to see the tables turned.

"In fact, we're thinking of putting her in a home," Loch continued, glaring at his grandmother. "She's a danger to herself and others."

"Why, I think your grandmother is delightful." Ginger flashed a smile at the sheriff. "I could come here every day. Especially if it meant more of this iced tea. And these brownies? Heaven."

"Yes, my grandmother sure can cook. Grandmother, we really need to be going. I've got work waiting for me back at the station."

"All right, but you bring your new girlfriend here any old time that you want. How about this Sunday? Sunday works for me."

"We'll see," he muttered. He glanced at Ginger, who was holding a brownie in front of her face to smother a laugh.

Ginger turned to Willie. "Willie, would I be able to take a few of these brownies with me? It's for a good cause."

"Certainly," she said happily, and grabbed a Tupperware box from a cupboard. She quickly put a dozen brownies in it. "There's more where those come from. You come by any time."

As they started to walk out the door, his grandmother put her hand on Ginger's arm. "Why did you turn my grandson down when he asked you to dance?"

Ginger paused, startled. "Well...it was the way he asked me. He just marched right up and barked 'Dance with me'... not even so much as a please."

Willie shot him a look, and cuffed him on the side of the

head.

"That is not how we raised you, Lochland Connall Armstrong."

He groaned and rolled his eyes. "Grandmother, please."

Ginger sighed. "Why can you get away with that and I can't?"

"Well, dear, as family I do have certain privileges. But he's the Alpha of our pack, so while I may chastise my grandson, I do it discreetly. And not in public."

"Point taken," Ginger nodded, and followed him out to his patrol car.

"That was delightful," she said as they climbed in the car. "Can we go there every day for a nice long lunch?"

"No, we cannot." He glowered. "Are you giving me a hard time? Aren't you supposed to be trying to please me so I give a good report to your Alpha?"

"You know, you've got all these women in town simpering over you and kissing your butt. I think I'm going to take a different approach." She buckled her seatbelt. "Can we go check on Cletus before we go to your office?"

"Sure thing. And don't think you're escaping punishment for your sassy behavior back there, young lady."

"Oh really? What did you have in mind?"

"Let's just say you're lucky you're not a member of my pack, because I'd likely put you over my knee."

A sudden image of her over the sheriff's knee flashed through her mind, and a wave of heat rolled over. She stifled a whimper.

In her mind's eye she was naked, and squirming, and he was firmly restraining her with one hand and bringing his other hand down on her bare buttocks.

She pressed her lips together tightly and tried to think un-sexy thoughts as they drove. Ashmont's image flashed through her mind. How they always had sex with the lights off. How he only liked it missionary style.

"Here we are," the sheriff said, pulling up in front of the community center, which was smack in the middle of the Main Street shopping district. They were on a big lot of land, set back from the sidewalk that led to all the little shops up and down the street. Like the sheriff's office, it had a big sign with the Blue Moon junction logo of a wolf howling at the moon.

They both climbed out of the car. "Can you follow my lead?" Ginger asked. "Just agree with whatever I say."

Cletus was in the garden, running his hoe through the dirt. He wore a handkerchief on his head.

"Hey, Cletus, glad to see you made it," the sheriff said. He glanced at the garden. "You made some good progress here. If this keeps up, I might be able to recommend you to the town's public works department for a full time job."

"Really?" Cletus looked startled.

"Swear to God. I'm impressed."

"By the way, Cletus, I thought maybe you could help me out with something. I'm trying to learn to cook, and I made these brownies this morning, but nobody will try them for me."

She pulled the Tupperware container full of brownies out of her purse and held them out to him, making a sad face. "Everyone says that city girls can't cook. Even the sheriff wouldn't try one."

Sheriff Armstrong sighed, but nodded. "Yep. That's true. I don't believe city girls can cook."

Cletus took the container of brownies, bit into one, and his face lit up. "City girls sure can cook! Wow. I got to find me a city girl."

"See? I told you!" Ginger flashed an ingratiating smile at the sheriff.

"Okay, I believe you. In fact I think I'll try one." He reached for the Tupperware container.

"You had your chance!" Cletus walked off quickly,

shoveling two brownies into his mouth at the same time.

"Nice one," the sheriff said in a low voice. "You have a way with people, Miss Ginger. You really do."

"Sometimes."

"Yep, sometimes. When you put your mind to it." Was it her imagination, or did he look a little hurt when she said that? Like he wished she'd put her mind to it for him?

His cell phone rang, and he glanced at the number and scowled. He grabbed the phone and answered it. "I'll be right back," he said to Ginger, and turned and walked to the edge of the yard.

Ginger walked over to Cletus. "So, is everything else going all right?"

"Sure is. I'm saving the other brownies for my brother and sisters." He smiled shyly. "You sticking around town, then?"

"Ahhh…" Ginger felt a sudden flash of guilt. She had a feeling that Cletus and his family really needed a friend. "I don't know. Maybe."

"Really?" His face lit up. "That would be nice. Not too many people around here will talk to me."

Crud. She'd gotten his hopes up. Why had she lied? She couldn't stay here. She had a job waiting for her back home – maybe. She had an overpriced apartment with a view of another apartment building's air conditioning unit. She had an aversion to walking in fields full of cow patties.

"You know, when I put those coins back in the fountain…I made a wish," Cletus said, staring down at the ground.

"Oh? What kind of wish?"

"I can't say or it won't come true." His face wrinkled anxiously. "You think the wish will still work if I was using stolen coins?"

"Well, you were actually returning those coins at that point, so, uh…maybe?" Ginger's heart ached for Cletus. What would he wish for? Clothing without holes in it? Food in the refrigerator?

"I better get back to work." He set the box of brownies down on the bench and grabbed the hoe.

A couple of well-dressed women walking by glanced at him, and one of them clutched her pocketbook closer to her chest.

"Isn't he that dirty Arbuckle boy?" one of the woman said loudly.

"Certainly is. I don't think he's had a bath in his whole life."

Cletus' face fell and he turned and began raking the dirt again, without a word. His eyes glittered with hurt and humiliation.

"Of course he's dirty, he's working in a freaking garden! Where there's dirt! Maybe if you ever did a day of work in your life, you'd have room to talk!" Ginger yelled after them.

They flashed her a shocked lock. "What are you looking at?" she snapped, and they turned and hurried off.

"Don't tell the sheriff I said that," she told Cletus. "I'm already in enough trouble with him."

"Join the club." Cletus was smiling now.

The sheriff strolled over to them, tucking his phone in his pocket.

"What was that all about?" he asked.

"Nothing," Cletus said.

"What he said," Ginger added. He gave her the skeptical eyebrow raise, but didn't say anything.

Ginger followed him to his car. "You looked a little perturbed by that phone call."

"It's nothing. Call from the council."

"The shifter council?" The wolf shifter council was a big deal. They oversaw all matters for wolf shifters in their respective state.

"Yes, that's right. Nothing to worry about. Anyway. We got to head out. There's trouble at the dig," he said.

CHAPTER SEVEN

To reach the dig, they drove down a joltingly bumpy country road for a mile and a half, until they finally reached a clearing by an old, dried up creek bed. There were several tents set up there, and outside the tents were tables and folding chairs, and a cluster of SUVs.

There was already a patrol car on scene when they arrived. Jax and another deputy were arguing with a group of panther shifters who were standing by a cluster of pine trees. The students were in the creek bed, sifting through dirt.

"You've got no damned authority here! None!" Jax was yelling at them. The shifter he was talking to, a tall muscular man with black flowing hair streaked with gray and white, who wore a traditional loincloth and buck skin boots, looked as if he were about to change form and throw down. Hair was bristling from the tips of his ears, and his eyes glowed yellow, as Loch and Ginger rushed up.

"Settle down, everybody. I'll handle this. Montgomery, what's going on —"

"These damned panthers"- Jax rushed in.

Loch spun on Jax with a growl, and his claws shot from his hands. His eyes blazed amber, and the bones in his face rippled and lengthened. Within seconds his face was covered with hair and his teeth sharpened into fangs.

For a brief second, Jax's eyes sparked with fury, but then he quickly backed down and went down on one knee, bowing his head.

"Sorry. Didn't mean to interrupt," he muttered.

"You'll wait in the patrol car."

"Yes, sir." Jax didn't look happy about it, but he obediently climbed to his feet and loped over to his patrol car without a backward glance. His deputy glanced at Loch for guidance, and Loch inclined his head towards Jax's car. "Go," he said in a low growl, and the deputy ran after Jax.

He turned back to Montgomery and made a polite incline of his head. "My apologies," he said. "My lieutenant spoke out of turn."

Professor Reese was standing there, arms folded, glowering at Montgomery. "No he didn't," he said petulantly. "Your deputy was right. This man has no authority over me. He can't tell me to do anything."

Montgomery glanced over at Ginger. "Who's this?"

"Ginger Colby." She thrust her hand out to shake hands with him. "I'm delighted to meet you. I've heard so much about the Panther nation. I teach a unit on them to my fourth grade class in New York, you know."

"I'm always happy to meet people who are respectful of our culture." Montgomery inclined his head politely.

The panther shifters who were standing with him came forward and made a point of shaking hands with Ginger, while eyeing her appreciatively. "Tommy Deerkiller," one of them said. "I own the souvenir shop. Come by any time."

My God, Ginger thought, I love it here. I am going to call all of my fat friends and make them vacation here with me, so help me God. This is chubby chick heaven.

She heard a low rumbling growl and glanced over at Loch, who seemed to be struggling to contain himself. Quickly, she stepped back. He wasn't actually jealous, was he? He couldn't possibly be jealous.

Although she found herself oddly flattered at the thought.

"These are my pride mates, Richard Iron Claw and his son Jason Strikes True." Montgomery nodded at two panther shifters who were standing by his side, muscular men with the shining black hair of their tribe pulled back into pony tails.

"Perhaps we could give her a tour of our property." Tommy smiled at her lasciviously. "Since she's so interested in our history."

"If she can go on your property, why can't a legitimate scientist?" snapped Professor Reese.

"Because you're not a legitimate scientist. You're a treasure hunting looter with no respect for indigenous people's customs," Montgomery snarled.

"So," Sheriff Armstrong said quickly, cutting them off. "What brings you out here today, Montgomery?"

"I demand the right to inspect his site and all of his vehicles for stolen artifacts," Montgomery said.

"Absolutely not. He may rule his Nation like a demi-god, but the second he steps out of the Nation's territory, he has no authority." Professor Reese folded his arms and looked smug.

"Why doesn't he want us to look at his dig? Has he got something to hide?" Montgomery glowered.

"Let me on your land, and I'll let you inspect our dig," the professor smirked at him.

"Panthers don't make deals with humans!" Montgomery roared, fangs descending.

"Show some respect for our leader, or pay the consequence!" Richard Iron Claw's eyes blazed with rage.

"This whole expedition is a fraud! He's not even a specialist in Mastadon fossils! He's a specialist in early Native American tribal lore, and he has a reputation as a thief of priceless artifacts!"

"I gather artifacts for museums! You're selfish! You hoard

them and hide them from the world!" The professor sounded like a two-year-old who'd been denied a new toy.

"They're our heritage! They're not trinkets for people to gape at!"

"I've never stolen an artifact in my life! Keep flinging false accusations at me, and I'll sue!" Professor Reese actually stamped his foot on the ground. He stood several steps behind the sheriff as he did so.

Ginger bit her lip in frustration. She was dying to jump in and yell at them as if they were all a bunch of kindergarteners, which is exactly what they were acting like, but to do so would be to undermine the sheriff's authority.

The yelling grew more heated, and she turned and walked away.

As the shouting reached a fever pitch, Jax and his deputy leaped out of the patrol car and came trotting back to stand behind the sheriff. Both groups of men glared and bristled at each other.

Several minutes later, the panthers turned, shifted into panther form, bellowed out a series of threatening roars, and turned and loped away.

The sheriff joined Ginger a few minutes later. He left behind Jax and the other deputy, parked in their patrol car.

As they drove away, Ginger said, "Okay, I get it now. You can't have anyone challenging your authority as an Alpha because then people like Jax think they can step up and challenge you."

"I'm glad you see that. Jax has been making rumbling noises, coming near to challenging me, for months now. He thinks that being diplomatic is the same as being weak. He wants to do everything by force. If I let him have his way, he'd start a war with the panther nation."

"Did I make things worse for you that night at the Hoot Owl?"

"Not too much."

"I promise I won't openly challenge you again."

"Openly?" he was smiling now.

"Oh, come on. I just don't have it in me to never give you a hard time. And it's even more fun when I'm being subtle about it."

"Speaking of giving me a hard time…did you yell at two old ladies who were walking by the community center? Portia called to inform me of it."

Ginger winced. "She really doesn't like me, does she?"

"She doesn't, but that's not the point."

"They were yelling insults at Cletus! Did she mention that? They totally made fun of him. And he didn't even say anything back to them; it was all me."

"No, she did not mention that. However, there are probably ways that you could have responded to them that would have set a better example for Cletus and reflected better on your pack."

She pouted as they rode in silence. She was right, damn it! She wished he could have seen the look on Cletus' face when they mocked him. Grown women, making fun of a skinny young boy.

Finally, grudgingly, she said, "If it will help maintain your authority, you can punish me for it publicly. However you see fit. "

His eyes lit up with a gleam.

"However I see fit? You sure about that?"

Her face flushed, the blush spreading all the way down to her toes. Her private parts were probably blushing. What did the devious sheriff have in mind? Nothing good, she was sure, but it was too late to back out now.

"Ahhhh….yes. I am a woman of my word. However you see fit," she choked out.

"All right." His smile turned sensual and his eyes had a gleam to them that worried her. "The punishment will take place tonight, after work."

Did this count as a date? Her mind flashed back to what Marigold had said about punishment and seduction…and how there was a fine line between the two of them.

Damn it! She hated it when Marigold was right.

She spent the rest of the day at the office, filing and answering phones, and trying to ignore the feeling of Portia's angry glare burning holes in the back of her head. At least Jax just ignored her, while Lola came and sat on her desk and peppered her with questions about New York City.

That evening, Loch dropped her off at the boarding house so he could go home and change.

Ginger was just in time to help Marigold pick out an outfit for her date with Henry. Marigold deliberately chose jeans and a tank top, to let Henry know she didn't think the date was any big deal.

Ginger looked her over and shook her head, frowning. "I hate to tell you this, but you look sexy as hell in that outfit, and Loch also told me that Henry really likes a girl in jeans. What he doesn't like is frou-frou city girls."

"Really?" Marigold stared down at her outfit in dismay. She quickly ripped her clothes off and threw on a low cut, clingy red dress that molded to her slim figure. She climbed into a pair of high heels and put on some sparkly lip gloss, and topped off the look with big gold hoop earrings.

"Ha! That'll repel him!" she said triumphantly, watching from the window as his car pulled up out front.

Ginger walked downstairs with Marigold. "By the way, I made all that up about the jeans," she told Marigold as Marigold stepped out on to the front porch. "And you look hot in that dress. Ay, caramba! Oops, he's already getting out of his car, you don't have time to change."

"What?" Marigold's eyes went wide with shock. "You conniving bitch!"

"You've known me for 8 years, and you're just now figuring that out? Heh heh." Ginger cackled an evil laugh and ran back inside the boarding house, leaving Marigold alone as Henry walked up the flagstone path to the porch.

A rustling in the hallway behind her made her start, and she turned.

Winifred was standing there, looking perturbed. As usual, she had her hair pinned up in the pencil-bun. "I was wondering…" she said, wringing her slim hands. "That new person employed by Miss Imogen to assist her with the daily tasks at this domicile…"

"The hot handyman? What about him?"

"Are you aware of whether he has any, er, involvement or marital commitment with a member of the opposite sex? Or the same sex?" At Ginger's startled look, she blushed and muttered "I'm asking for purely academic reasons."

"I don't know. You should ask him. But try to say it in normal-speak, or he won't understand you. Just say, by the way, do you have a girlfriend? And if he says no, ask him if he'd like to buy you a drink at the Hoot Owl."

"Really?" Winifred's eyes widened at the thought.

"Absolutely. It's the 21st century. Sisters are doing it for themselves." As Winifred opened her mouth to demand an explanation, she held up her hand. "That's an expression! It means, it's okay for a girl to ask a guy to ask her out on a date."

"Interesting. Very interesting."

"Hold on." Ginger reached out and grabbed the pencils out of Winifred's hair bun, and handed the pencils to her as her golden locks tumbled down over her shoulders.

"Never do the pencil thing again," Ginger told her. "Especially when you're talking to the handyman." She reached out and unbuttoned the top four buttons of Winifred's oxford shirt. "Okay, now you're good."

Winifred nodded, stuffing the pencils into her shirt pocket. "Thank you. This has been a most illuminating conversation."

She wandered back into the house with a thoughtful look on her face.

Loch pulled up a few minutes later, sexy as sin in jeans and a white t-shirt. Ginger still wore her floral pink skirt and scoop neck shirt.

"Should I have changed?" she asked nervously, as they drove.

"You look beautiful."

Her heart leapt in her throat. Her palms were damp with sweat and she struggled to control her breathing. Right now she was both terrified and fascinated by the sheriff, and so turned on that she wanted to tear her clothes off and crawl on top of him.

Down, girl, she told herself.

"Where exactly is this punishment taking place?" They were driving out of town, down a dark country road with no illumination but the glow of the moon and the car's headlights.

"Now, why would I tell you and spoil all of my fun? Besides, the anticipation's part of your punishment."

"You're kind of a sadist, you know that?" she grumbled.

"Is that right? Think about that before you smart-mouth someone, next time." He was grinning hugely, enjoying himself way too much.

He took her down a small country road and into a wooded cove, to a non-descript warehouse style building. There were several dozen cars in the dimly lit parking lot.

"What is this place?" she asked him as they climbed out.

"It's a private, members only club. I wanted to bring you here for a couple of reasons. I know you tend to bristle at authority sometimes, that you think I'm too dominant and overbearing."

"Sometimes," she muttered, blushing.

"I wanted to show you that being dominant isn't all bad. It

has its place, and its purpose. It can be very…pleasurable under the right circumstances."

She stared up at him. Did he mean what she thought he meant? Was it…that kind of club?

Her heart was beating a million miles a minute, and she felt moisture soaking her panties. She didn't bother to fold her arms over her nipples, which were swollen and straining against the fabric of her t-shirt, two sensitive pink nubs that yearned for Loch's mouth to suck on them.

"I…" she was speechless.

"But if you don't want to go in, that's all right too. I would only want you to go in if you feel comfortable doing it."

She swallowed hard.

"Will you be with me the whole time?" she asked, her heart hammering against her rib cage.

"Of course. Every second. I wouldn't leave you."

"I want to go in," she breathed.

She followed him through the doorway, in a daze.

They walked down a long hallway, and inside, they stepped into a very large open room.

A room that was a dominant's heaven. And a submissive's too, for that matter.

There were padded benches and pommel horses and restraint stations of all type set up around the room. Chains dangled from the ceiling. On the walls were racks holding floggers and paddles and ball gags. The lighting was low and red-tinged. Music drifted from hidden speakers, an ominous instrumental soundtrack that Ginger didn't recognize.

Muscular men in leather were enthusiastically punishing women who were tied down in various positions…and the women were moaning with pleasure.

The sheriff glanced over at her. "You okay with this?"

"I…yes. I mean, I've never done anything like this, but…yes."

Her voice was husky with desire. She was surprised with

how okay with it she was. More than okay. The idea of Loch tying her to one of those frameworks and caressing her with the leather tendrils of a flogger...she let out a small involuntary whimper of desire as she pictured it.

"I'm glad I'm your first." His eyes twinkled as he looked down at her.

"Me too. I trust you. I couldn't do this with anyone else," she told him, looking around the room.

She suddenly realized that she recognized someone...Jax. He was stripped to the waist, revealing magnificent muscles. His partner was a beautiful redhead, naked except for a tiny g-string and a pair of spike heels. Her hands were tied together and stretched above her head, as she dangled from an overhead chain. Jax was standing back, flicking at her back with a rawhide whip that left red stripes criss-crossing her back.

With every strike of the whip, she let out an orgasmic cry.

Loch skimmed his fingers lightly over Ginger's back, and she shivered and bit her lip, her breath quickening. "This way," he said.

He led her over to a wooden frame that had metal rings fixed to it at strategic places, with ropes dangling from them, and he positioned her by two of the metal rings.

Then, he tied each wrist to a rope and adjusted them until her arms were stretched over her head. She was facing the wall, with no idea of what he'd do next. The anticipation made her shiver. She wanted his hands on her so badly, wanted to feel his muscular body crushing her up against him...

He grabbed the waistband of her skirt and pulled it down until it lay on the floor, puddled around her ankles. She was wearing pink lacy hipster underwear that exposed most of her generously sized rear end.

He ran his fingers slowly over the skin of her right butt cheek, fingers lovingly tracing the ivory globe. Trails of pleasure sizzled in the path of his fingers, shooting through all the nerves in her body, down to her fingertips and toes. Her pussy throbbed with need. She bit back a moan and squirmed where she stood.

"You're going to count out loud for each stroke," he told her. She glanced back and realized that he was holding a paddle in his hand, and she tensed in anticipation. "If you don't count, then the stroke doesn't count. Got it?" His voice cracked through the air, stern and authoritative.

"Yes," she whimpered.

Please. Do it, she thought.

"Yes, what?"

"Yes, sir."

Suddenly she felt a sharp thwack on her right butt cheek, and felt mingled pleasure and pain sizzling through her body.

"One!" she cried out quickly.

"Louder. You get nine more strokes," he said. He swung the paddle again, and she cried out, letting out a moan. "Two," she cried out. He moved to a different spot and smacked the paddle onto her butt check. "Three," she yelled, dancing in place.

Again, and she could feel the hot blossom of pain blooming where he'd struck, but it felt so right.

"Four!"

"Still not loud enough, Ginger."

He moved the paddle again, and she gasped out loud as it struck her sensitive flesh, and glowing embers of pleasure bloomed inside her. "Five!"she yelled at the top of her lungs.

"Ahh, that's much better. You're learning," he said.

"Yes, sir! Thank you, sir!" she called out, loudly.

"Very good, Ginger," he said in a voice grown husky with desire, and then traced his fingers over the spot he'd just struck.

He knelt down behind her and ran his tongue along her stinging flesh. "Mmmmm," she moaned, not even trying to hide her pleasure any more as he caressed her heated skin with swirling strokes of his tongue.

Then he stood up again, and resumed paddling her. Each strike sent lightning bolt of pleasure jolting through her body. She whimpered in pleasure, a ball of heat curling up in her abdomen.

"Five!" She clenched her teeth. When the paddle made contact with her bottom, the pleasure shot through her entire body, and she could feel heat pooling in her abdomen, below her navel. Her nerves were alive, crackling with desire, craving the sting of the paddle.

He was going to make her come. Right here, in front of everyone.

There were a crowd of men and women watching now, and she was breathing hard, gasping with pleasure.

Oddly she wasn't self-conscious. Maybe it was the way the men looked at her here, as if she were incredibly sexy and they were turned on just by looking at her.

Several more paddle strokes and she couldn't help herself. The final paddle stroke sent her over the edge. "Ten!" she screamed, and she felt the ball of heat explode inside her, shooting sparks throughout her body, and wave after wave of orgasm swept through her. She whimpered and shuddered as she dangled helplessly from the ropes. "Oh, oh, oh," she gasped. Her panties were absolutely soaked.

When Loch untied her, she moaned with release and slumped into his arms. He held her up easily, his muscular arms wrapping around her, and she breathed in his scent, desire already rising inside her again. More. She craved more. She pressed herself against him, loving the feeling of his steel-hard muscles, the tightening of his arms.

What would he do to her next? The flogger? Nipple clamps? There were so many parts of her body that he hadn't punished yet.

"Put your skirt on," he commanded in a low growl. She

bent down and quickly pulled her skirt back up. Her backside pulsed from the swatting she'd just received; she felt as if her skin were glowing red right through the cloth.

Suddenly she found him moving her quickly towards the door.

"Hey, Loch, can I play with her now?" A leather-clad wolf shifter stepped up eagerly, blocking their path.

Loch replied with a growl that raised the hair on the back of Ginger's neck, and the shifter leaped back, alarmed. Loch rushed her through the front door and into the parking lot.

She stood there in the warm, humid, night air, bewildered and shaken.

"What…what's wrong?" she stammered.

"Give me a minute." Loch staggered back several steps. He was breathing hard, his eyes were glowing amber, his ears had started to lengthen and turn pointy. She could see him struggling to regain control of himself.

"What is it?" she pleaded. "Was it something I did wrong?"

A man walked up to them and looked Ginger up and down. "Nice, Loch. Would your new playmate like a threesome?"

Suddenly Loch shifted into wolf form and leaped through the air, knocking the man down and snarling and snapping at his throat. The man shifted into wolf form as well, crying out and waving his paws in the air.

Instead of backing off, Loch stayed where he was, his jaws snapping inches from the man's throat, and the man cringed, howling in fear.

My God, he's going to kill him, Ginger thought.

"Loch, stop!" she screamed.

Loch shifted back into human form, breathing hard.

"I'm sorry," he groaned. "I shouldn't have done that."

He rushed her into the car, panting for breath and shaking.

They rode in silence back to the boarding house. The whole way there, she could see him shifting between wolf and human, struggling with the wheel. The car jerked on the road and she clutched at the door in alarm, pressing herself back against the seat.

When they got to the boarding house he let her out with a tortured groan.

"It was a mistake," he growled, burying his face in his hands, which were covered with fur, thick black claws curving out. "Bringing you there. It was a mistake."

CHAPTER EIGHT

Ginger lay in bed, stripped naked, burning with desire and head whirling in confusion.

Did the sheriff have feelings for her?

Apparently not. Apparently he regretted his very public scene with her.

Damn it…she wanted him so badly she couldn't even think straight. Her brain was fogged with desire.

She gripped the rubbery shaft of her vibrator, closed her eyes, and, shamefully, pictured the sheriff in her mind. It hurt to want someone who didn't want her.

She imagined herself naked, lying on this bed. Tied down, arms and legs secured to posts. He'd be on top her, straddling her…

She pressed the vibrator against her tiny, tight opening and worked it in, moaning wordlessly as she slid it in and out. Picturing his thickness, she felt heat gather inside her again and then sweep over her, pulsing to the ends of her fingers and toes. It wasn't the same, though; her orgasm felt dull and muted, and left her aching for the feeling of Loch's arms crushing her against the broad wall of his chest.

That night she tossed and turned for hours, tormented by vague dreams she couldn't remember.

The next morning, apparently everybody was out of sorts. Marigold looked tired and sulky. Brenda and Tallulah sat glaring at each other. The professor didn't even bother to show up.

And even Winifred was unusually quiet, although Ginger caught her staring out the window at the handyman, who was outside repairing a fence. At least she wasn't doing the pencil thing any more, and she'd unbuttoned her shirt a couple more buttons, so she was actually showing a wee bit of cleavage.

Halfway through breakfast, Brenda threw down her napkin and stood up. "I'm going to go get the professor," she announced. "He never sleeps in like this. Maybe his alarm clock is broken."

"No, I'll go!" Tallulah jumped up.

The two stood there, glowering at each other.

"Oh, for God's sake! I'll go, because I assure you, I have no interest in the professor whatsoever." Ginger snapped, and turned and headed up the stairs, with Brenda and Tallulah on her heels.

She knocked hard on the professor's door. There was no answer.

"Professor! Hey, professor!" she yelled.

Still no answer.

She reached down, turned the knob and pushed the door open. She could see the professor's bed from where she stood. The handmade quilt was tucked in, the bed was neatly made, and the professor was nowhere in sight.

"Oh my God. He never came home last night!" Tallulah gasped.

"He was at dinner. What are you talking about?" Brenda protested.

"No, last night after dinner I was in the back yard when I saw him headed out. I asked him where he was going and he said he forgot something at the dig, and he'd be back later. Something must have happened to him!"

Ginger felt uneasiness roiling in her stomach. After yesterday afternoon's confrontation, and with the heated emotions that had been stirred up, she wouldn't be surprised to hear that he'd come to harm. Maybe the panther shifters had come back to check the site for stolen artifacts, and he'd surprised them?

She glanced at her watch, and was surprised to see that it was quarter after 8. The sheriff had picked her up promptly at 8 a.m. the day before.

And he hadn't called. That didn't seem like him at all.

She felt an iciness creeping over her. Apparently, this was it. He'd briefly flirted with the idea of seducing her…and he'd found the idea unappealing.

Last night, she'd sort of let herself hope that his violent reaction at the club was jealousy. Obviously it wasn't. Maybe it was embarrassment.

Her cheeks burned with humiliation at the thought, and she hung her head, blinking back sudden tears and turning away from Tallulah and Brenda.

Apparently not everyone in Blue Moon County was attracted to fat chicks, she thought bitterly.

Brenda put her hand on her arm. "You were in love with him, too, huh?" she said sympathetically.

"The professor? No! Absolutely not," Ginger spluttered. Her head was whirling. She could have called the sheriff to see why he hadn't come for her – he'd given her his cell phone number – but stubborn pride kept her from doing so.

She took a deep breath and let it out slowly. It did nothing to diminish the dull ache that throbbed inside her chest.

Focus, she scolded herself. We've got a possible missing person here.

"Can one of you try to call the professor?" she said, and Tallulah and Brenda both whipped out their cell phones and dialed at the same time. Ginger rolled her eyes. Everything had to be a competition with those two.

Both of them got his voice mail.

"Okay. I'm going to drive to the sheriff's office and see if he's in. If he's not there, I'll call him and let him know about the professor not coming home last night," she said.

When she went back downstairs, Marigold gave her a quizzical look. "Everything all right? Not working today?"

"Can I borrow Imogen's truck to go to town? The professor went to the dig last night to get something he forgot, and he never came home."

"Oh. Good heavens. Yeah, go ahead. And if sheriff jerkwad hurt your feelings, I'm going to punch the fuck out of him," Marigold added. "Of course he'll probably kill me afterwards, but it'll feel really good while I'm doing it."

"I thought he was Sheriff Sexy-ass?"

"If he upset you, he's Sheriff Jerkwad."

Ginger forced a smile. "Everything's fine. No punching. No name-calling. I'll call you from the sheriff's office."

As she drove to the office, her phone rang, and she grabbed it quickly. Her heart sank when she saw that it was her Alpha's number.

"Ginger? How is everything going there? You haven't caused any more trouble, have you?" Reynaldo's tone was aggrieved.

"Everything is going fine," she said brightly.

"Are you sure? You sound strange. What have you done now?"

"Nothing! Everything is going really, really well. Oh, gotta go! Another call's coming in." She hung up quickly.

When she pulled up out front, she saw that the sheriff's patrol car wasn't there yet. Now unease rippled through her stomach, warring with anger and hurt.

She walked inside and saw Jax sitting at his desk. He

glanced up at her, his expression neutral. "Do you know what time the sheriff is coming in?" she asked.

"No. He called and said he'd be in a little late." He went back to his computer.

Oh. So he'd called Jax, not her. So at least he was all right…he was just making it quite clear that he wanted nothing to do with Ginger.

Her heart thumped painfully in her chest. First Ashmont, then Loch. Rejection was becoming painfully familiar these days.

Should she turn around and go back to the boarding house? But that would make it too obvious to everyone there that something was wrong. And it might make Loch look bad, as if she'd disobeyed his orders and was ditching her assistant duties.

Portia, sitting at a nearby desk, flashed a cold smile that dripped with malice. "Oh, trouble in paradise?" she asked sweetly.

"Cut it out," Lola snapped.

"Or what?" Portia's eyes glowed.

Lola leaped up from her desk and whirled to face her. "Or, get up off your bony ass and you'll find out what-"

"Lola! I need help finding a file on my computer! Could you show me?" Ginger said desperately. The last thing she needed was to be accused of starting a fight right in the middle of the sheriff's station.

Grumbling, Lola followed her, shooting dirty looks over her shoulder at Portia, who bared her fangs and let out a long, low growl.

Jax was sitting at his desk, typing away on his computer.

Ginger sighed, took a deep breath, and walked over to him.

"The professor never came home from his dig last night," she told him. She hated to tell Jax, because she didn't want to stir up trouble between the wolves and the panthers, but she had the feeling that the sheriff didn't want to hear from her.

It surprised her how much that hurt. It hurt far worse than when Ashmont had texted her to tell her it was over. This was like a bruise that spread all through her insides, deep and aching.

"What do you mean?" Jax looked up, his brow furrowing.

"He didn't come down to breakfast this morning, so we went and checked his room. It was empty and his bed hadn't been slept in. One of his students told me that she saw him after dinner last night, and he said that he was going to head out to the dig to get something he forgot. And apparently, he never came home."

"Which student?"

"Her name is Tallulah."

Jax waved one of the other deputies over. "All right. We'll head out to the dig right now. Thanks," he said, and headed for the door, muttering "Freaking panthers."

Ginger felt unease ripple over her. There was no way Jax would approach this situation with any diplomacy – but after the way the sheriff had flipped out last night, she doubted he was in any better mood to deal with it either.

She walked back to the filing room to resume her filing. It was nearly impossible for her to concentrate; she could barely remember the alphabet.

A little while later, Portia came and knocked on the door.

"The sheriff wants you at a scene," Portia said, her expression neutral.

"What kind of scene?"

"Death that was just reported this morning. It appears that the body's been moved. We want to find out what happened during his final moments. Come with me."

Portia turned and walked out of the room without looking back.

Ginger scrambled to follow her, head whirling. The sheriff

wanted her to go with Portia? That was hard to believe. Then again, it was also hard to believe that the punctual sheriff had never showed up to pick her up this morning, and hadn't even bothered to call her to explain what was going on.

Her heart sank. He really didn't care what happened to her.

Silently, she climbed in the car with Portia. "Where are we going?" she asked as she shut the door.

"You'll see when we get there," Portia said coldly, and took off with a lurch as Ginger was buckling her seatbelt, so fast that Ginger slammed into the dashboard in front of her and then was slammed back into her seat.

Portia's lips curled into a small, cold smile as they headed out of town.

After several minutes of driving, Portia suddenly took a turn down a narrow country road that was shaded by trees.

Ginger's unease grew, and she wondered how much longer she should put up with this silent treatment before demanding answers. Could she even demand answers? Would this get back to her pack somehow, and get her in even worse trouble?

Frustration curled inside her, and she folded her arms across her chest, scowling.

"What's the matter?" Portia asked snidely. "Don't like the country? Then you're in the wrong place, sweetheart. You should get back to the city where you belong."

"I agreed to serve as the sheriff's assistant for two weeks. I intend to keep my word," Ginger said, in a cool but neutral tone.

"I should think it would be fairly clear by now that the sheriff has already lost interest in you. You could leave town right now and he wouldn't even notice." Icicles dripped from Portia's words. "In fact, you should. You're just embarrassing yourself, panting after him like a lovesick pup."

Was that true? Ginger wondered. She knew that Portia

was bitterly jealous of her – but still, after the way the sheriff had vanished, Portia's words stabbed at her.

"You know, it's obvious to everyone that you're incredibly out of place here," Portia continued. "A red wolf in a gray wolf's territory. A half-breed running with an Alpha. Didn't anyone ever tell you it's dangerous to leave the safety of your pack?"

The car slowed. Suddenly Portia's eyes were glowing amber, and the bones of her face began to shift and lengthen. Thick black claws shot from her finger tips.

And that was that.

Ginger had had it.

She'd grown up being bullied, taunted for being different, for being fat, for being weird, for talking to people only she could see. And, back in middle school, she'd finally gotten tired of it. She was never the type to start anything – but she'd sure as hell finish it.

Her foot shot out and slammed on top of Portia's foot, jamming on the brake so hard that the car skidded and bounced on the road before screeching to a halt.

"What the hell was that?" Portia shrieked, as Ginger's fangs sprang out and hair sprouted on her face.

"That was me saying I've had enough. You're obviously counting on the fact that a typical red wolf is half the size of a gray wolf. Well, I'm not a typical red wolf, in case you hadn't notice." Her voice came out in a snarl.

Portia stared at her, frozen in shock, her eyes widening.

"I've got a good eighty pounds on you in human form. You want to find out how big I am when I turn? You want to find out how we deal with bullies in New York? Step outside of the car and let's settle this." Ginger opened her door and gestured at the road.

Portia just kept staring, breathing hard, and finally she turned back to the road, started up the car again, and said in a cold, quiet voice "Please close your door."

Ginger slammed the door shut, hard.

"You and I are done speaking to each other," Ginger snapped. "I don't want to hear another word out of you while we're in the car. Drive me to this scene, if there even is a scene, and let's get this over with."

Portia's face darkened with anger, but she didn't say a word. She made a u-turn, drove back to town, and soon they were in a high end subdivision, driving past mini mansions surrounded by massive sprawling lawns.

They pulled up in front of a Tudor style home, with a steeply pitched roof, rubblework masonry and decorative half-timbering. There was an ambulance parked out front, a deputy's car, and a hearse.

They walked up the flagstone path and climbed the steps in silence. Two life sized statues of stone wolves sat on either side of the doorway, signifying that these were wolf shifters. Wealthy wolf shifters.

Inside, in a spacious living room, a small crowd had gathered. A woman in a two piece Chanel suit and shiny black pumps sat on the couch, dabbing her eyes with a handkerchief. A young man was holding her hand. Several well-dressed couples who were probably her neighbors sat on the overstuffed leather sectional, murmuring words of support.

There was a deputy sitting in a chair with a laptop on his lap, tapping away as he wrote his report. They all glanced up when Ginger walked in.

"This is Ginger Colby, sheriff's office liaison. She's a certified post-death communications expert," Portia announced loudly. "She'll be able to communicate with the deceased about his final moments."

The woman in the Chanel suit blanched.

"Well, I really don't think that's necessary..." she protested.

"After everything that she's just been through!" one of the other women on the couch said indignantly.

"It's routine." Portia threw a glance at Ginger. Everyone was staring at Ginger with open hostility, and Ginger glanced back at Portia, to see that cold little smile playing across Portia's lips again. The smile vanished as soon as Ginger's eyes were on Portia, and her face went carefully neutral.

"Follow me, please," Portia said, and lead Ginger down a hallway and into the couple's master bedroom. It was a large room decorated in dark gray and black tones, with black lacquer furniture.

A corpse lay on the bed with a sheet pulled over him.

"The rigor mortis and livor mortis in the body shows us that he didn't die in the position that we found him. He'd been dead for several hours, and then somebody moved him. But the wife is insisting she came home from her garden club meeting this morning and found him in exactly that position," Portia said.

Ginger sighed, taking a deep breath.

She closed her eyes, letting the world disintegrate around her, and when she opened her eyes she could see a man with curly silver hair on the bed – and he wasn't alone.

The silver haired man was mostly naked, on his hands and knees, facing the edge of the bed. He wore a leather harness held together with metal rings.

Standing by the bed was another man – a muscular young man who had pulled his pants down around his ankles. The silver haired man had the younger man's cock in his mouth, and was enthusiastically fellating him – when suddenly, he collapsed, face down and buttocks in the air, still in the kneeling position.

The younger man jumped back in shock. Then, grimacing, he reached out tentatively and shook the older man by the shoulder, and shouted his name several times.

When he couldn't rouse him, he quickly pulled his clothes on and fled without a backward glance.

The silver haired man abruptly sat up and looked straight at Ginger. Sometimes the dead did that. Sometimes they just played out the scenes of their death, again and again.

"My wife can't know," he said. His eyes were huge and hollow.

Ginger shook her head, clearing her thoughts, and the room returned to normal. No ghosts, no final death scene.

Her hands were shaking. She turned and walked quickly out of the room, with Portia following at her footsteps.

"Well?" Portia said loudly, glancing around the room. Everyone stared at Ginger with a mixture of anger and fear.

It was likely they all knew about this man's double life, or at least suspected. And Ginger would lay odds that the body on the sheet had been stripped of the leather harness and repositioned before the police were called.

Ginger took a deep breath. Portia knew exactly what had happened, and she'd set Ginger up to be the bad guy.

If it were necessary, Ginger would have announced the truth, but there was no need to humiliate this man's family. The man hadn't been murdered; he'd died in the middle of sex.

"Death by natural causes," Ginger said coolly. "He appears to have collapsed and died from a heart attack." She turned to the widow. "I'm very sorry for your loss."

There were audible sighs of relief from the widow and several of the people sitting with her.

"What?" Portia's voice cracked angrily through the room. "Remember…you're certified! You are sworn to tell the truth!"

"I am telling the truth," Ginger said coldly. And she was. It appeared that the man had died of a heart attack. She didn't need to mention what activity he was indulging in when he had that heart attack.

"If you lie during an investigation, you will lose your certification!"

"You think that the coroner's office is going to find some other cause of death besides a heart attack? He wasn't shot, stabbed, strangled, or poisoned…he collapsed," Ginger said firmly. "I'm not a doctor, but I know what I saw. He collapsed. And never regained consciousness."

Suddenly Portia looked around the room and realized that all eyes were now on her. All the people in the room who'd been glaring at Ginger were now glaring at her.

Her gaze dropped to the floor, and she shot Ginger a dirty look.

"We'll just see about that," she mumbled angrily.

"Portia Sinclair, what the heck is going on here?" Loch Armstrong's voice rang through the air.

CHAPTER NINE

Loch had come into the house un-noticed, and was standing in the arched entryway to the living room, his face dark with anger.

Portia's face went pale. "Outside. Now," he snapped.

Portia swallowed hard, then turned and stalked out of the house without a word.

The sheriff nodded at the widow. "I'm sorry for your loss, Miss Timmons," he said, and turned and walked out, and Ginger followed him, her heart frozen in her chest. What the hell was happening here?

Portia was quickly climbing into her patrol car when the sheriff barked at her "Get back here, now!" She froze and sat there for a second as if contemplating the idea of ignoring him, then she slowly climbed out and walked over to where he stood, her face sullen.

He glanced at Ginger. "What are you doing here?"

"Portia said that you wanted me to investigate…" she saw Portia frantically gesturing at her as if begging her to be quiet. Obviously Portia had lied when she'd said the sheriff wanted Ginger at the scene.

The sheriff turned to Portia. "Are you crazy? You thought you'd get away with going behind my back like that?"

Portia didn't answer, staring sullenly at the ground.

"We all know what happened with Mr. Timmons. There was absolutely no need to humiliate that woman and her family like that. You brought Ginger here to stir up trouble and make her look like the bad guy – at that family's expense."

"I didn't say anything to the family," Ginger said hastily. "I just said that it appears that he collapsed and died of a heart attack. Which is true. Mostly. I mean, there was a young man in the room with him when he collapsed, and they were, uh…"

"I can imagine," the sheriff said darkly.

He turned back to Portia. "I should be out dealing with a missing professor, and preventing Jax from starting a war with the Panther Nation. Instead I'm here dealing with your childish and completely unacceptable behavior."

"Unacceptable!" Portia hissed. "I'll tell you what's unacceptable! She's a red wolf, you're grey! You can't-"

The sheriff let out a low, warning growl, and his eyes glowed amber with rage.

Portia wilted, shrinking back. "You can't treat me like this. You know who my aunt is," she muttered weakly. "I'll quit, that's what I'll do."

"Resignation accepted. Ginger, come with me." He turned on his heel and walked away, with Ginger quickly following him.

Portia's wails of protest filled the air. "You can't do this! You'll hear from my aunt! You'll hear from the council!" she shouted.

Ginger and the sheriff climbed into the patrol car. Ginger had to hug herself to keep her hands from shaking.

The sheriff pulled out of the parking lot. "I apologize for that. And for this morning. I owe you an explanation," he said. "Portia...her family has been trying to arrange a marriage between us for ages, for political reasons. Their family is very wealthy, mine has a lot of connections and influence in this area of the state. I made it very clear to them that she wasn't my fated mate, but they kept pushing . A year ago I took her out on a couple of dates, and then I broke it off. She didn't take it well. She managed to get herself hired at the sheriff's department by having her aunt pressure the mayor, and she's constantly trying to meddle in my personal life."

"Who's her aunt?"

"A member of the Shifter Council."

"Oh. Good lord." The seven member council oversaw all matters concerning the various werewolf packs in Florida. Each area of the state had a representative. Every state had a council, and their word superseded that of the Alpha, if they felt that an Alpha was acting against the interests of his pack.

"Don't worry about it. The real issue is...what happened between us last night." He was breathing hard, and Ginger stared at him. He looked disheveled, his hair rumpled and a twig caught in his hair. She reached out and plucked it from his hair without thinking, and he let out a low groan at the feel of her fingers.

"Did you shift and run in the woods before you came here?" she asked him.

He rubbed at his face with one hand, the other hand clenching the wheel so tightly that his knuckles were white.

"I had to," he groaned. "I ran for hours. I felt like I was burning up. Like I was going to explode."

She stared at him. "What, exactly, is going on with you?"

"Last night, at the club...I scared myself."

"You scared me too. And that wolf who made a pass at me outside the club."

His eyes blazed angrily at the mention of it, and he took a deep breath, and then pulled over to the side of the road. "I've never reacted like that before with anyone. I've taken plenty of women to that club before, and I didn't care who else played with them. Who they fooled around with. But you...the thought of any other wolf laying his paws on you, any man touching you...it literally made me crazy."

Ginger's heart leaped to her throat, choking her. Loch wanted her. And he didn't want any other man to even come near her.

"I wasn't going to fool around with anyone else," Ginger said. "I only want you." As soon as she said it, she bit her lip. She hadn't even realized she was going to say it, hadn't even realized that she meant it, until she heard herself saying those words.

"I mean..."

He took another deep breath, clearly struggling for control. "We need to go out to the dig site right now and deal with the missing professor. Can we talk about it after that? Please?" The normally dominant Alpha was begging her, in a low, sexy growl.

Ginger's panties suddenly were soaked with the juices of her desire. She squirmed in her seat and bit her lip. She could feel desire pulsing between her legs and jolting through her body.

"Yes," she said huskily. "We can talk about it whenever you want."

"Good God, woman. You have no idea the effect you have on me. Can you try not to talk in that sexy voice?"

"Umm..." she lowered her voice to a comical bass pitch. "Is that better?"

He threw back his head and laughed. "Much better."

They drove to the dig site, where several patrol cars were parked. Jax was standing with a group of deputies, glaring at Montgomery. Montgomery was pacing back and forth like an angry cat. A dozen other panther shifters were milling about, and they were clearly angry.

"Sheriff," Jax said. "There are ATV tracks leading from

the site into the woods. We were waiting for you before we follow the tracks."

The sheriff nodded. He glanced at Montgomery. "We'd appreciate if you'd accompany us, Montgomery. To ensure that we don't accidentally encroach on your territory."

Jax glowered, looking as if he were about to argue, but then his shoulders sank in defeat and he shrugged angrily. "Fine," he muttered.

"I'll be back," the sheriff said to Ginger. "Wait here for me." She nodded her assent.

The men all strode to the edge of the wood, and then shed their clothes, leaving them in piles. She watched as they shifted, sinking down on all fours, snouts lengthening, fur sprouting, tails lashing, and then dashed into the woods.

The students were milling around uncertainly, not sure what to do. Some of them sat inside a tent they'd set up, drinking bottles of water and muttering among themselves.

About half an hour later, the shifters returned, shifting quickly and changing back into their clothes. The panther shifters left immediately, headed into the woods, and the sheriff and his deputies trotted over to where Ginger sat inside the tent with the students.

"The ATV tracks lead into panther nation territory," Loch said. "Unfortunately we have no authority there."

The students let out a chorus of protest. "We need to find the professor!" "They murdered him!" "That's not fair!"

"I'm going to go back to speak to Montgomery tomorrow to see if I can convince him to let us come onto their territory, after he's had a chance to calm down," Loch said, shooting Jax a dark look. Jax scowled at the ground. Clearly, Jax had exchanged words with the leader of the Panther Nation, and clearly, it had not been well received.

"Does he admit they murdered him?" Brenda's eyes were glittering with tears.

"No. He denies any knowledge of the professor's

whereabouts. He says he was unaware that the professor came onto their territory until just now, when we saw that the ATV tracks led there."

"So you're going to just give up?" Tallulah wailed.

"No, we're not going to just give up. My men are going to need to take statements from all of you. I'm also going to have to go through the professor's room to see if there's any indication as to why he'd go into Panther territory when he knew the consequences," Loch continued. "And if I need to, I can contact the Panther's shifter council to see if they'll intervene. But we're not there yet. Montgomery can be reasoned with as long as he's approached respectfully." He fixed Jax with a hard look before turning away to head back to his patrol car.

It was hours before Loch had finished taking statements and searching the professor's room.

Ginger went back to the sheriff's office and finished up the filing, while the sheriff sat in his office and fielded phone calls from North Florida University where the professor taught, family members, the mayor, the town's newspaper reporter, and others.

Loch confided in Ginger that the last time the professor had used his phone had been about half an hour after he left the boarding house…and it had been right outside the Panther Nation's territory. According to cell phone tower signals, the person who answered the phone had been inside the Panther Nation.

Unfortunately, the person he'd called had used a disposable cell phone that was untraceable. Neither the professor's cell phone, nor the person he'd called, were returning any signals now.

In the professor's room, in a hidden compartment in his suitcase, they'd found a research paper about a feared shaman who'd ruled the panther nation several centuries ago, and who had practiced magic so dark that his own people had risen up against him and assassinated him.

"The Shaman, who was called River Runs Red, had turned to virgin sacrifice and black magic. He used that magic to create what were believed to be icons of great power and great evil," Loch told Ginger. "There were some sketches included in the research paper, showing what the icons are believed to look like."

"Those kind of icons would be very valuable, wouldn't they? And terribly dangerous if they got in the wrong hands?" Ginger said.

The sheriff's expression turned somber.

"What?" she asked.

"There have always been rumors that those icons can't be destroyed, that they still exist deep within panther territory, and that's why they're so territorial, why they never let outsiders on their lands. They believe that if anyone were to get their hands on those icons, it would unleash unspeakable evil."

Something about the way he said it sent a cold shiver rolling down her spine.

"But there's no way the professor could get to them. He'd have to know that. It would be absolute suicide for him to even attempt it." He shook his head.

"The professor is far from suicidal," Ginger agreed. "And he knew how the panthers felt about him, and about any attempts to remove their ancestral icons from the territory. But…it sounds as if you thought he had an inside man."

"We do. But how would an inside man get him past all of the other panthers? It still doesn't make sense."

He ran his hands wearily over his face. "Okay. The day's over. Let's go for a run. I need to clear my head and then we can talk."

They drove outside of town, and the sheriff pulled into a small wooded cove by the side of the road. Loch got out of the car and Ginger followed suit, shutting the patrol car door.

He walked over to stand next to her, and she felt that familiar tingling sensation rolling over her, the pulse of desire that throbbed inside her with each heartbeat. "Talk to me," Ginger said.

"Ever since the first time I laid eyes on you, I wanted to claim you as mine," Loch told her. "That's why I went all caveman on you at the Hoot Owl. I've been trying to fight the urge to grab you and rip your clothes off every second that I'm alone with you."

Ginger stared at him in amazement. Several long seconds ticked by as she tried to process what he was saying.

"Why me?" she asked finally.

"Why? Because you're beautiful, and smart, and kind, and sexy, and because you give me a hard time when nobody else dares too, and because you're my fated mate."

"I…what? You believe in that? In the city, we think that's kind of a myth."

"Of course we believe in that," Loch said. "It's true. My grandmother was with her fated mate for seventy years until he passed away, God rest his soul. My mother and my father, too. They live north of here; you'll meet them."

"But…I just met you."

"Don't you feel it too?" He took her hand in his, his eyes pleading. The feeling of his skin brushing against hers set her senses on fire, and she bit her lip, stifling a whimper.

"I don't know what I feel. Every time I'm near you, I tingle all over and I can barely concentrate and everything I say sounds stupid and…" she was blushing and staring at the ground.

"Have you ever felt that way about anyone else?"

"Never."

"Listen, this isn't the olden days where the Alpha drags his fated mate off to his homestead the second he scents her, and there's a shotgun marriage on the spot," Loch assured her. "Although, let me tell you, those marriages always lasted.

That's how my grandfather claimed my grandmother, in fact."

"What?" Ginger's eyes widened in surprise.

"This is the 21st century. I get that. We can take all the time you need. And there'll be courting. Plenty of courting." His voice dropped to a low growl. "But no other men."

"And no other women!" she protested, and then wanted to smack herself. Was she agreeing to this? Had she gone completely crazy?

"Of course, no other women." At her skeptical look he added, "I know my reputation. But I've literally never been serious with any other woman before I met you. And I've never lied to a woman . All those women that I was with…it was like I was trying to fill a void while I was looking for the one."

"Oh." Her eyes were round with wonder.

"Let's run," he said.

CHAPTER TEN

Quickly, they both shed their clothing and shifted.

Ginger's senses blazed to life, the glorious scents and sounds of the forest swirling around her as they dashed through the woods. She could smell rich loamy earth and the scents of every kind of tree and the berries on bushes, and the sun warmed her fur as she followed Loch.

He weaved through the trees, leaping over bushes and logs, and they ran and ran until they finally came to stop by a stream bed. Loch bent over the bank and dipped his head to drink, and Ginger did too, their long pink tongues curling the ice cold water into their mouths. There they both shifted again, and stood naked on a bed of moss by the running water.

With a growl, Loch swept Ginger into his arms as if she were light as a feather, and then set her down gently on the moss bed. He grabbed her wrists and pinned her arms above her head, sliding on top of her. His muscular body was covered with a sheen of sweat, and he was breathing hard.

"Just so we're clear…in bed, I'm always the dominant." His voice rumbled out, deep and sexy.

"I gathered that," she said, between panting breaths. "I like it."

He moved down, his lips pressing against hers, nibbling at her lower lip, and she let out a whimper of pleasure. Then his mouth moved on hers, and her lips parted, accepting him. His kiss was hungry and demanding, his tongue probing, exploring.

The weight of his body felt delicious. Everywhere his skin touched hers, she could feel her nerves sizzling. The thickness of his erection pressed between her legs and she moaned and parted her thighs.

He began kissing her neck, nipping at it hard enough to make her gasp with delight, then running his tongue over the tingling skin in long, slow laps.

He moved down to her breasts, kissing them and cupping them in his hands, and then sucked her swollen, sensitive nipple into his mouth and teased it with his teeth.

"Ohhhhh," she wailed. "Yesss….like that…" He scraped his teeth across it and she gasped her pleasure. He moved to her other breast, tongue swirling in circles around the pink circle of her aureole, and then closed his mouth around her nipple and sucked hard.

Hot waves of pleasure snaked through her, and she tangled her fingers in his silky curls, caressing him. She could feel the warm rays of the sun beating down on them, and the trilling of birds was like a symphony.

When he moved down lower to kiss her rounded belly, she flinched and tried to move away. He grabbed her hands and pinned them by her side.

"Stop," he growled. "I love your curves. They're what make you a woman. Let me show you." His tongue swirled in circles on her stomach and dipped into her navel, and her breathing quickened, coming in short, sharp pants.

He slid down further, spreading her fleshy thighs apart

with his hands, and kissing and nipping at the curves of her flesh.

Then he was between her legs, caressing the dewy wet petals of her pussy, spreading them open. "Ohhhh," she wailed. "My God. Like that. Just like that."

She would have done anything for him. The hot waves of pleasure felt like rivers of lava now, burning her with unbearable ecstasy. When he sucked the swollen rosebud of her clitoris into his mouth and scraped his teeth over it, she screamed aloud, in pleasure so intense she thought she'd die.

Loch was merciless, his hands spreading her lips wide apart and his mouth sucking hard, teasing, nipping, until she couldn't bear it no longer.

She felt as if the earth fell away from her and she writhed beneath him, shuddering violently with the force of her orgasm. She lost all sense of time and place, vaguely feeling him sliding up on top of her and kissing her neck as he positioned himself on top of her.

"Inside me," she moaned. "I want you inside me."

"Like this, baby?"

Loch moved his hips, and the head of his cock nudged between the wet pink petals of her pussy.

She wailed, moving to accept him, and he forced his way into her tight tunnel, sliding in several inches.

"Harder," she gasped.

"Shameless hussy." He thrust again, deep inside her, and she grabbed his butt cheeks with both hands, fingers sinking into those perfect, muscular globes.

"Oh my God, you're so tight. Yes," he groaned, and began moving his hips, pistoning into her rhythmically. He'd pull back, almost sliding out of her, and she'd moan with anticipated loss, and pull him back in.

His hips moved faster and faster, and his breath was harsh and quick, searing her ear as he groaned in pleasure.

She felt that heat inside her again, curling inside her pelvis, bunching up so tightly that it was as painful as it was pleasurable, and then she could hold back no longer, and she wrapped her legs around him and pinned him in place, plunged deep inside her.

The ball of heat shattered and sent shards of ecstasy shooting through her body. She let out a long, low moan and felt the sheath of her muscles clenching convulsively, clamping hard on his cock, and with a groan of pleasure he exploded deep inside her, his body shuddering as he joined her in climax.

Afterwards, when his breathing had slowed and his body had stilled, he cupped her face in his hand and turned her head so she was staring up into his eyes. His beautiful brown eyes, which were glowing amber with passion.

"Say you're mine," he commanded.

"I'm yours," she whispered, heart beating a thousand miles a minute.

He nipped at her lower lip.

"Say I'm the only one for you." He growled it into her mouth, and she let out a little moan of pleasure.

"You're the only one for me."

"And you for me." He gathered her into his arms, crushing her up against him.

"I feel…That burning inside me, that madness that took over me, it's…better. It's lessening. As long as I have you with me, I'm all right," he rasped.

"I'm with you," she promised.

She felt him relaxing, and gradually his breathing slowed until it matched hers, and they were breathing in rhythm.

"We should get back," she sighed, glancing at the sun sinking below the horizon. "The professor…everyone will be waiting and wondering. I wish we could stay out here forever."

"We have forever," he whispered in her ear, his breath tickling her. "We'll have all the time in the world."

He reluctantly let go, sliding off her.

The two of them shifted again and dashed back through the woods, the cooling night air delicious in their fur. When they reached Loch's parked patrol car, they quickly shifted back and changed into their clothing.

As they pulled to a stop in front of the boarding house, Loch suddenly turned to Ginger. "Come spend the night with me," he pleaded.

She hesitated, biting her lower lip. "I want to, more than anything. But this thing with the shifter council…that's no joke. I think we should keep this on the down low for a little while. Let people get used to me."

He let out a low growl of frustration.

"All right…for now," he said reluctantly. "But I don't know how much longer I can wait to publicly claim you. I'm on fire when you're not with me. My wolf claws at me from the inside."

"I know," she groaned, and reached for his hand. He pulled it away, clenching it into a fist. "If you touch me and I know I can't have you…" His voice were harsh and his eyes dark and gleaming.

She nodded, and swallowed hard. "Soon. A few more days. Let's give it a few more days. Maybe Portia will calm down and get over it." Somehow, she doubted it, but she didn't think it was a good idea for her and the sheriff to rub their relationship in Portia's face right after Portia had basically been booted out of the sheriff's office.

She climbed out of the car and headed back to the house.

Marigold and the students were all in the sitting room, and they looked up anxiously when Ginger walked in. Ginger shook her head. "I'm sorry, guys. There's no news."

The students faces fell, and they went back to muttering among themselves.

"You missed dinner, but we can reheat something for you in the kitchen," Marigold said. "And by the way, you're going to tell me absolutely everything."

"You first. What about you and loverboy?" Ginger said, following.

Marigold shrugged, looking unhappy. "We went out. He was very nice to me. He's funny. He kissed me good night and he's a great kisser."

"So?" Ginger grabbed a plate from the refrigerator and carried it over to the microwave.

"So, I already told you what I saw as our future."

"But-"

"No buts," Marigold grumbled. "My mother's been divorced six times. She's getting ready to marry number seven. I'm an expert in how relationships end. That's why I try to avoid them."

"So you're not going to see him again?"

"Well, after he kissed me I found myself agreeing to let him cook me dinner at his place tomorrow night. I guess after dinner, I'll tell him it's over."

Ginger shook her head, sighing. "You're being ridiculous, but I can't live your life for you."

Under much prodding from Marigold, she gave her a g-rated description of her afternoon with the sheriff, including the fact that the niece of the local Council member had it in for her.

"What a bitch," Marigold shook her head.

"You don't know the half of it. I don't know, I'm still… I'm so confused about everything. He says I'm his fated mate. He's so completely different from me, this town is so different than everything I've grown up with, but it feels so right."

"If it came right down to it, you could teach here just as well as you could teach in New York. I'd come visit you here."

"Do you think that the whole fated mate concept is really a thing?"

"It's a thing," Marigold nodded solemnly. "A thing that I'll probably never have. If he says that he's your fated mate, then you are. The sheriff may be many things, but he's not a liar. I can tell. Why fight it?"

Ginger fell asleep that night with a deliciously satisfied ache between her thighs, and was woken up early the next morning by a pounding on her door.

With a groan, she made her way across the room and yanked the door open.

The archeology students were standing in the hall.

"Is it true that you can communicate with the dead?" Brenda demanded.

"The professor." Ginger smacked her forehead with her hand. Of course. She should have tried to communicate with him as soon as it was established that he was missing. She'd been so distracted by Loch that it hadn't even occurred to her.

"Have you heard from him? From the other side?" Tallulah's voice came out in a high pitched wail.

"No, it doesn't work like that. I have to be at the scene of their death, or in their home, or somewhere that they spent a lot of time. Sometimes it works if I just touch something of theirs, a physical object that they've touched. Somewhere their psychic energy would be lingering, so it opens up a pathway for me to communicate with them. And over the years, I've built up my mental defenses to the point where I actually screen out the other side most of the time; I need to be concentrating, and focused, to communicate with the dead."

"Well, let's go then!" Brenda said impatiently, arms folded, tapping one foot in a nervous staccato.

"Let me call the sheriff first and get his okay."

"No, now!" Brenda tried to push her way into Ginger's room.

"I said I need to call the sheriff," Ginger said firmly, shutting the door in their face and locking it. Brenda immediately began knocking on the door loudly, yelling "Hey! Hey!" over and over.

"Shut up! Let her call him!" Tallulah yelled.

Sighing, Ginger dialed Loch's number. He answered immediately. "Good morning, beautiful. Did you sleep well?"

The warm, rich sound of his voice made her tingle pleasurably.

"Good morning to you too. I slept very well. Listen, there's something I should have thought of. If I go into the professor's room, I can try to communicate with him. Maybe I can get an idea of how he died."

"My God, I should have thought of that."

"We were both a little distracted."

"Wait for me. I'll be there in about 20 minutes."

She shivered in anticipation, and prayed she wouldn't act like a complete dork when he pulled up. She was in the middle of a possible murder investigation, and she still felt hot and tingly all over at the sound of his voice. She must be a complete pervert.

Quickly, she dressed and left the room. The students followed her down the stairs, with Brenda haranguing her the whole way.

"You have to go up there right now! It can't wait! We have a right to know!" Brenda wailed as Ginger sat in the dining room and sipped coffee that Marigold had bought for her. Brenda and Tallulah were standing behind her, breathing down her neck. Winifred and the other students were at the table, picking at their breakfast, distracted, along with the other boarding house lodgers.

"Actually, no, you don't," Ginger said irritably. "You're not a family member."

"We were very close," Brenda sniffed, blinking back angry tears.

"Sure you were. Your vagina was, anyway," Tallulah muttered.

"Jealous bitch!" Suddenly the two of them were jostling, bumping into Ginger, making her slosh coffee on the floor.

"Cut it out!" Ginger snapped.

"All right, settle down, ladies." Loch was standing in the doorway with Jax. Ginger's heart did a funny little happy dance in her chest, despite the grimness of the situation, and she flashed him a smile.

As Ginger, Loch, and Jax started to head up the stairs, the girls tried to follow. They grumbled when Loch shook his head, and clustered together at the bottom of the stairs, muttering.

Loch walked in the room with her while Jax stood outside.

In the professor's room, Ginger sat down on his bed and closed her eyes, consciously relaxing, slowing her breathing.

When she opened her eyes, she was startled to realize that she felt…nothing.

She glanced up at Loch, startled. "He's not dead," she said.

CHAPTER ELEVEN

"Are you sure?"

"I would sense it if he was. He might not communicate with me, but I'd at least sense his presence on the other side. He is not there. He's still alive."

Loch looked at her in consternation. "Then the panthers must be holding him prisoner somewhere on their property. That's the only explanation for his disappearance. I've got to talk to Montgomery today."

Ginger nodded. "If he says you can't come on their property, then what?"

"I've always found Montgomery to be a reasonable man, as long as he's approached respectfully. I'm pretty sure that if I talk to him later today, he'll let me on the property. If they deliberately harm the professor, or if the professor disappears on their land forever, it's bad publicity for all of them. People won't want to visit their stores or their casino. It will be devastating economically."

As they drove to the sheriff's station, her cell phone rang. Wedding march ring tone. She grimaced.

"Answer it, Miss Ginger." When she made a face, he said

sternly, "Answer it. I'm the Alpha. Unless you want to be punished later."

"Of course I want to be punished later," she grinned, and hit talk.

"How are things progressing with the sheriff?" her mother said. No hello; she cut straight to the chase.

"Just fine, mother. No war is imminent."

"I'm debating whether you'd look better in white or cream. What do you think? Maybe even pink. You've always looked lovely in pink. Also, I'd been thinking about a wedding cake made of cupcakes, but that may be passé'."

"Mother! I just got here! Quit drinking the crazy juice!"

"Also, do you think the wedding would take place in New York or Florida?"

"Love you, mother. I'm at work, so I can't talk. Bye." She hung up quickly. "Crazy. She's crazy."

"What, because she thinks you should marry me?" he said with mock hurt.

"Come on! I just got to town, we agreed we'd take it slow…"

"Hmmm," he grumbled. But he didn't say anything else as they headed to the station.

As they pulled into the sheriff's parking space, Loch groaned aloud.

Reporters from all over the state were blocking the entrance to the station. Ginger dodged past them and dashed inside as the sheriff held an impromptu press conference, reassuring them that everything possible was being done to find the missing professor.

When Loch went inside, Lola greeted him apologetically. "You've got a few million messages," she said, handing him a stack of pink "While you were out…" notes. The professor's disappearance, and the Panther Nation's refusal to cooperate, was getting massive amounts of attention.

Loch had to place a dozen calls to people inside the Panther Nation before he finally heard back from an assistant to Montgomery. Montgomery agreed to meet with the sheriff that afternoon, at the entrance to the Panther Nation's property.

Around mid-morning, Ginger asked Loch if he could have his grandmother make them some sandwiches, with a few extra for Cletus.

"We'll go over there for lunch. It'll win me some major points with her," the sheriff said.

His grandmother was waiting on the front porch for them when they pulled up, with a plate piled high with sandwiches. She set the sandwiches on a table on the porch.

"She just gets prettier every time I see her," Willie said Loch as they sat down to eat, and then she went inside to get them some lemonade.

"I swear she's measuring my hips with her eyes," Ginger whispered to Loch. He grinned.

"Your mother and my grandmother. We should get them together for coffee some time."

"Good lord, no. My mother would show up with a wedding dress, a priest and a shotgun. And your grandmother would probably have a giant butterfly net, a bible, and some flower girls. What is their rush?"

"Well, you're not getting any younger." He winked as he said it. She still kicked him in the ankle.

"Careful there, darlin'," he said. "Respect the Alpha. You haven't seen how hard I can spank when I'm truly motivated."

The thought sent delicious shivers rolling through her body. His hand on her bare naked buttocks…

Willie walked out with a pitcher and two glasses.

"That's very thoughtful of you to feed that Arbuckle boy. Poor thing," Wille said with a sigh, as they drank their lemonade. "I hear his mother ran off a couple weeks ago. Just up and left the whole family."

"Oh?" the sheriff raised an eyebrow.

"No!" Ginger said quickly. "You can't have his brothers and sisters taken away from him! He's got a job now."

"He's not 18 for another six months. Legally, there needs to be an adult in that house."

"If you take them away, you take away his incentive to work, to straighten out his life. Have a heart," Ginger pleaded.

"I'll think about it. But my ultimate duty is to uphold the law." He didn't look happy.

Her phone jangled, and she recognized the number as her Alpha's. She stood up and walked away from the table, clicking the "talk button". She was ready to accept the lavish praise he'd heap on her for saving the day and improving relations between the Gray and Red wolf packs.

She'd be humble about it, of course. Nobody likes a gloater.

"Are you completely off your rocker?" Reynaldo hissed into the phone.

"What?" she gasped, shocked.

"Don't you 'what' me. I just heard from a Florida council member, Aurora Sinclair. She says you're just about ready to start a war down there! She says you're offending absolutely everybody with your boorish behavior, and they want you out of town immediately! I expect you on the next train back to New York, and when you get here, you are in serious trouble. As is your family."

"She's lying!" Ginger turned pale.

Willie and Loch both rushed to her side. "What is it?" Loch demanded.

"It's my Alpha," Ginger managed to sputter, weakly. "Aurora Sinclair told him that I'm offending everyone down here and –"

Loch grabbed the phone from her, his face like thunder.

"This is Loch Armstrong. What did you just say to my fated mate?"

Ginger's eyes widened with surprise at his public declaration.

"Goodness, what took him so long to realize it?" Willie whispered.

Ginger could hear Reynaldo spluttering on the other end of the phone, stammering out apologies.

"Aurora Sinclair does not speak for my pack. Our pack has been delighted with Ginger's company, and we are hopeful that she'll consider our offer to permanently relocate down here. You may consider Ginger to be under my protection."

More spluttering from Reynaldo.

"I don't care that Aurora's a member of the council. She is the only one who's unhappy with Ginger's presence here, and that's because she's trying to arrange a marriage between me and her niece. If you have any problem with what I'm saying, you may name the Challenge location of your choice."

Reynaldo's spluttered quickly changed to apologetic mewling.

Loch hung up, and turned to Ginger. "How did that man ever become Alpha?" he asked, amazed.

"It's different in New York."

"Obviously."

Ginger managed a weak smile. "Thank you for defending me."

Loch peered at her with concern. "What's wrong?"

"Council members have a lot of power. She could cause you a lot of harm. For that matter, she could cause my family a lot of harm. I know she's a member of the Florida Council, not New York, but still…"

Loch shook his head angrily. "She won't ruin what we have. I won't let her. Nobody is taking you from me."

"But it doesn't affect just you. Depending on what action she takes, it could affect the whole pack. And my parents. My father has worked for the Alpha for years, and if he were fired from that firm…my parents have a mortgage and three more kids to put through college."

Willie laid her hand on Ginger's arm. "Believe my grandson when he says that he won't let her take you from us. Everything will work out fine."

Hot tears of gratitude burned Ginger's eyes. Willie had said "us". As if Ginger belonged there.

Could it be true? Ginger had never really belonged anywhere before. Not all wolf, not all witch, with her large size always outing her as a genetic anomaly who straddled two worlds.

But the very fact that these people were so kind to her was the reason that she should leave town, she realized with a sinking heart. A vengeful council member could cause all kinds of grief for a pack.

"We should go," Loch said, draping his arm protectively around Ginger's shoulders. "We have work to do. Let's concentrate on that."

She nodded, and tried to force a smile on her face. When Loch had his arm around her, she felt so safe and protected. She felt as if she were exactly where she'd belonged. The thought of walking away from him made her feel small and cold and alone.

They headed over to the community center. Cletus was standing there talking to Elmore Bishop, the center director, while two little girls and a little boy played on the jungle gym. They were coyote shifters; clearly they were Cletus' younger brother and sisters.

The sheriff frowned when he saw them. Ginger shot the sheriff an indignant look.

"There's got to be an alternative to foster care," she said. "Besides, you have enough on your plate as it is right now. Can you just give it some time? Their mother could come back."

Privately she wished she could track down their mother

and smack her upside the head for what she was doing to her family, but she put a big smile on her face, walked over to where Cletus stood, and handed him the plastic box of sandwiches.

"I'm practicing my sandwich making skills now," she told him. "You need to test these out for me. Everything going okay?"

"It's going great. Mr. Bishop here said I could stay on and help out with the maintenance. He said I did a real good job," he said, with an undertone of defensiveness, as if he expected her to challenge him.

"Of course you did," Ginger said soothingly, and he relaxed a little.

"Sheriff Armstrong doesn't mind me bringing my brother and sisters here, does he?"

"Nope. It's fine," she said firmly, praying she was right.

The sheriff dropped her off back at the office. "I'm headed out to speak to Montgomery now," he told Lola. "I'll be back shortly."

Jax stood up from his desk. The sheriff turned to him and shook his head. "You're not coming with me," he said. "You are not to speak to any of the panthers until you learn some diplomacy."

Jax let out a low growl of displeasure. "We need to take a firm line with the panthers. They're making us look weak."

"Following the law, and the boundaries of their nation, isn't weakness." The sheriff stood up straight, his eyes taking on a warning glow. "It's respect."

"The species that deserves respect is the one that proves its strength," Jax snapped, his shoulders hunching up defensively. "The only way to earn respect is by establishing who's top dog. You're letting the panthers-"

"Enough!" Loch roared, and everyone in the room fell silent. "I am the Alpha. You do not argue with me. If you want to hold a Challenge, we can do it right here, right now.

Otherwise, you're on desk duty. Permanently. And if I hear of you challenging the panthers, or my word, again, you face expulsion from the pack."

Jax's eyes blazed with fury, and his body shook with the effort of restraining his inner wolf. His muscles swelled and rippled, and Ginger held her breath for what seemed like forever, before Jax finally nodded his ascent.

Clearly furious, he walked stiffly back to his desk, sat down, and turned his computer on.

"Do you want me to come with you to meet Montgomery?" Ginger asked.

Loch shook his head.

"No, it's best if I go alone. I know how to handle him."

The sheriff came back an hour later, his face was creased in a frown.

"I don't know what's gotten into Montgomery," he said to Ginger. "He really wasn't himself today. He says we absolutely can not come on to panther nation territory. And he's still claiming that there's no sign of the professor on their land. That's got to be a lie. By now, with all the hoopla around the professor's disappearance, they would have searched the land thoroughly. They would have followed the professor's tracks to wherever they ended."

"So what now?"

"We're working on figuring out who the professor's inside man was. We've got some leads, but I can't discuss them yet."

The Panther Shifter council were still considering the matter, and hadn't given the sheriff an answer yet. Loch confided to Ginger that he suspected they were going to stall for as long as they could. They were being placed in a difficult and politically uncomfortable position. They were supposed to do what was best for the panthers, but what was best in this case?

Over-ruling Montgomery's decision would be perceived as an attack on his authority – but the refusal of the Panther

Nation to allow anyone to look for the professor was hurting the reputation of all the panthers.

Towards the end of the day, Ginger's phone rang. Her father was calling.

Worried, she quickly answered. These days, phone calls from home never seemed to bring good news.

"Ginger, what is happening down there?" he asked, his voice shaking. "Reynaldo is talking about laying me off. Saying he can't afford to have me associated with his firm, with the way my daughter's behaving. What is going on?"

"What? Oh my God. I'm so sorry." Her heart sank. She could just picture her father, pacing in the living room. He was a small, perpetually anxious man, with thinning red hair and worried little eyes peering out behind gold-rimmed spectacles. He was the kind of man who lived for his family, who worried about their safety all the time, who tortured himself by calculating the statistical probability of every possible disaster that could happen to them, from getting salmonella from a bad tomato, to getting hit by a meteor. He worked overtime so his daughters could do to private school and college. The desk at his office was crowded with pictures of him, Ginger's mother, and his four daughters.

She looked across the room, at Loch sitting in his office. He was so handsome, so perfect, so right for her…and she was going to have to say goodbye to him.

"Dad, I'll fix this," she promised. Her eyes burned with tears as she hung up the phone and walked over to Loch's office. Her stomach churning, she opened the door.

"Loch, we need to talk," she said.

CHAPTER TWELVE

"You've got to stop her!" Tallulah said, grabbing Ginger by the arm.

Ginger cursed under her breath. After what had happened yesterday, she was not in the best of moods. She was trying to make her way to the dining room, but clearly she wasn't going to get a chance to eat breakfast.

Tallulah was standing there blocking her way.

"What? Who am I stopping?"

"I mean, she's a bitch and a whore, but I don't want her to get herself killed," Tallulah added.

"Oh. Brenda. What is she going to do?"

"She said she's going on to the Panther Nation territory to find him herself!"

Ginger rushed into the dining room to find Brenda in a heated argument with one of the other students. Brenda swung towards Ginger. "You said that he's still alive, right?"

"Yes. Most definitely."

"Then I'm going to find him," Brenda said defiantly, and turned and strode towards the door.

"No, wait!" Ginger pleaded. "The professor went on their

property, and disappeared. What do you think they'll do to you?"

"I don't care." Brenda's chin quivered and her eyes swam with tears. Her eyes were bloodshot and ringed with runny streaks of mascara and eyeliner. "None of you even care. None of you are doing anything to help him."

That wasn't true, but Ginger knew it was pointless to argue.

"Listen," she said, "Let me go talk to the panther nation's souvenir shop and talk to Tommy Deerkiller. Maybe he'll listen to reason, or have some ideas on how to talk to Montgomery. He's the one who stands to lose the most from this, because the disappearance is going to hurt the tourist industry.

"You promise you'll talk to him today?" Brenda sniffled, wiping at her cheeks with the back of her hand.

"I'll go right after breakfast."

After she ate, Ginger got the keys to the pickup truck and headed over to Tommy Deerkiller's. She had an uneasy feeling that this wouldn't sit well with the sheriff.

After the phone call from her father the day before, she'd told him that she needed to go back to New York right away. He'd begged and pleaded, and finally she'd told him that she'd give it a couple more days and think about it, but she'd asked for the day off from work to clear her head.

The truth was, she was trying to build up her resolve to leave town, but she couldn't do that if she was working twenty feet away from Loch's office. Her heart melted and her shirt wanted to unbutton itself every time she looked at him.

The souvenir shop was located on Rural Route 220, right near the entrance to the Panther Nation property. It was a weather-beaten, one story wooden structure with a picture of a snarling panther on the billboard sign out front. "Authentic Panther Nation Souveneers!!!" the misspelled but enthusiastic sign advertised.

There were necklaces of fangs and claws, painted pottery, hand-made leather and wood drums, moccasins, packages of venison jerky, and thousands of other knick-knacks and odds and ends cluttering the shelves inside. Tommy Deerkiller was stocking the shelves when she walked in. He lit up at the sight of her.

"Well, if it isn't the beautiful red wolf," he said. "How may I serve you today?"

"Actually, I came to talk to you about Montgomery," she said. "I'm worried about what's going to happen if he continues to refuse to allow us to investigate the professor's disappearance."

"I agree," Tommy nodded, frustration creasing his forehead. "People will be afraid to do business with us. Our sales are already down, because of it."

"Is there any way that you could persuade him to reconsider? Sheriff Armstrong has always been very respectful of the panthers, from what I understand. Maybe if Sheriff Armstrong went on the property by himself?"

Tommy frowned. "Normally, I'd say yes. The problem is, ever since the professor's disappeared, Montgomery has been acting…different. Not himself. There's no talking to him or reasoning with him. Frankly, a number of us are concerned."

"What's he doing that has you concerned?" Ginger felt a ripple of unease shudder through her.

"A lot of things," Tommy said vaguely. Clearly he was uncomfortable discussing it.

"So what could you do about it?"

"We're debating that. But don't say anything to anybody; challenging Montgomery or going over his head isn't something that can be done lightly," Tommy said, lowering his voice and glancing around fearfully. "If you could tell the sheriff that we're working out how to address the matter, and ask him to be patient?"

"I could try." If Loch was speaking to her.

At the sound of a truck pulling up outside, they both glanced out the window. It was Montgomery's pickup truck, and he had two young women in the front seat with him.

"I better go," Ginger said. Tommy nodded, looking worried. "Not a word," he said to her anxiously.

"Of course."

As she walked out, Montgomery saw her and waved at her from the truck window.

She paused, waiting as he climbed out and walked over to speak to her.

"How are you doing, Ginger? Come to buy some souvenirs?" he asked cheerfully. It was as if he had no idea there was a potential war brewing and he was the cause of it.

"I'm fine, thank you. How are things with you?"

"Can't complain. So what brings you to our territory?"

She took a deep breath and thought fast. "I was looking for you, actually."

"Really?" he looked delighted at the prospect. "Would you care to join me in a drink? We could go to the Panther Lodge, if you like."

"On Panther territory?" she asked, startled.

"Certainly. I know you'll be respectful of our property and our people. And I'd love to introduce you around." He glanced at her with a gleam in his eye and a curve to his lip, his gaze roving over her body.

Good heavens, he certainly acted differently when Loch was around, she thought. Should she go? Maybe it was a way to encourage friendlier relations with the Panther nation.

Then again, he was acting downright flirtatious. Exactly how friendly did the panther leader want to get with her?

Ginger never had a chance to find out, because at that very moment, the sheriff pulled into the parking lot, and he did not look happy.

He glanced over at Montgomery, and nodded at him.

"You're needed back at the office," he told Ginger. "It's urgent."

She smiled apologetically at Montgomery. "Perhaps some other time," she said.

"Any time at all. You know where to find me."

She climbed into the sheriff's car, baffled by the odd change in Montgomery's demeanor.

As they pulled out of the parking lot, the sheriff snapped "What the hell was that? He was flirting with you!"

Ginger nodded, bewildered. "He was, wasn't he? That was a really strange encounter."

"Why were you even talking to him?"

She related what had just happened that morning, and the sheriff shook his head angrily. "That was a terrible idea, Ginger. By the way, Tommy Deerkiller is the one that we suspect of being the professor's inside man."

"What?" Ginger gasped. "I had no idea!"

"I can't tell you everything that's happening with the investigation. You shouldn't have gone out there without consulting with me first."

"You're right. I'm sorry. I was worried that Brenda would go onto the panther's territory and they'd kill her or kidnap her, like they did the professor."

"I don't think they would. The professor was deliberately antagonizing them, and he clearly went on their property to steal artifacts. That wouldn't be the case with Brenda." The sheriff sighed. "Not that it would be a good idea to have her go on their property when tensions are running so high."

Ginger suddenly realized that they were driving down an unfamiliar road, headed for the driveway of a blue clapboard bungalow-style house.

"Where are we?" she asked.

The sheriff blinked in surprise. "Oh. I took you to my house. I wasn't even thinking."

He parked the car in front of his house and turned to her,

exasperation on his face. He grabbed her hand, and at the touch of his skin she felt the familiar sizzle of attraction burning through her. "I just can't think straight when I'm around you," he said, his voice hoarse. "I barely slept last night."

She swallowed hard. "I'm sorry. I really am. I'm just trying to protect my family, and keep the peace with my Alpha."

"I'll talk to him again," Loch said, his hand closing around hers. "I can't let you go. You're what I've been looking for all of my life. You're like the puzzle piece that I didn't realize was missing." His thumb moved across the back of her hand. Ginger's breathing quickened, and heat flared between her thighs.

She glanced at the house.

"So," she said. "Here we are. At your house. Just you and me."

"I'd be rude if I didn't offer you a guided tour," he said.

"Yes, that would be very rude."

"Just a quick tour," he promised. She followed him into the house, cursing her complete lack of willpower. Loch was harder to resist than chocolate, and that was saying a lot.

The sheriff's house was decorated with a spare, masculine style, with handmade wooden furniture and a deer's skull with antlers over the flagstone fireplace. A floor to ceiling window looked out on a riot of tropical greenery, with red flowering hibiscus splashed in a blaze of color amidst orange trees and palmettos.

"It's beautiful," she said.

"It could use a woman's touch," he said, bending to kiss her neck, and then nipping it gently. "Know any women who might be interested in helping me redecorate?"

She laughed. "I imagine there's no shortage of volunteers."

"I have very particular tastes. She'd have to be a sexy

redhead with a smart mouth and a good heart and a very voluptuous body. And a fondness for spankings."

Loch pulled Ginger up against him and hugged her, hard. "You were a very bad girl, going to the souvenir shop without asking me first," he murmured in her ear.

"Yes, I was." Ginger's voice was husky with desire. "Are you going to punish me?"

"Walk over to the couch." He released her and stepped away.

Legs trembling with anticipation, she walked over.

"Now bend over the arm."

She did as he commanded, lying with her head turned to the side, face pressed against the sofa cushion, and her buttocks raised up in the air. She could feel the deep ache of need pulsing between her legs, and she let out a low, helpless moan. Waiting for him was sweet torture.

The sheriff grabbed the hem of her skirt and yanked it down, and then did the same with her underwear.

He slid his hand between her legs and began caressing her, fingers lightly skimming the lips of her pussy.

She let out a little whimper and shifted her weight, opening her legs wider.

His fingers probed deeper, and she drew her breath in between her teeth in a sharp hiss of pleasure.

Then his free hand descended on the round ivory globe of her right butt cheek, delivering a stinging smack.

"Oh," she cried out, and his fingers moved faster on her pussy, strumming her clit, playing her like an instrument, as he spanked her again. And again. The stinging sensation was delicious, and she squirmed with pleasure, whimpering with each smack. His hand moved to the other cheek, warming the skin with each stinging slap, and she quivered beneath him, struggling to catch her breath.

"You just love to be punished, don't you, Ginger?" His voice was hoarse with desire.

"Yes," she moaned, "Oh, yes."

The heat rose up inside her and then broke and flowed over her in hot waves. She clutched at the couch, fingers sinking into the fabric as she wailed her pleasure and the orgasm shuddered through her body.

"Don't move," he commanded, and she heard him fumbling with his belt and his pants, and then she felt the thick head of his cock sliding between the slick, wet petals of her pussy.

With a savage thrust, he speared her, forcing himself several inches inside.

She clutched the couch harder, knuckles turning white. "Yes," she moaned, and he grabbed her hips and thrust again, sliding all the way in and holding her firmly.

"I'll never let you go," he said, and drew back to thrust again.

"Oh, God," she whimpered, face down on the couch. He pumped harder, and she felt the tickle of his pubic hair against her buttocks, and the slapping of his testicles against her bare skin.

He slammed into her so hard that it rocked her body with each thrust, and she put her hands flat on the couch and braced herself, pushing back against him. She wanted all of him, wanted him to bury himself inside her to the hilt. He was so big that she could barely contain him, and she loved it, loved how it felt to squeeze his stiff cock with her muscles.

His breath grew harsher and faster, and his hands tightened on her hips, holding her firmly in place as his groans of pleasure reached a crescendo. His hot, sticky seed flooded inside her, and she felt his body shuddering with the force of his orgasm.

Finally, slowly, he pulled out of her with a groan. He pulled her up and spun her around, taking her into his arms, crushing her up against him.

"We can work this out," he told her. "Stay here with me, Ginger."

She wrapped her arms around his waist and pressed up against him, breathing in his scent, the smell of sweat and cologne mixed with the sweet scent of sex.

Her heart swelled in her throat, with an aching longing. In his arms she felt warm and safe. The thought of walking away her sent icy shivers through her.

"I want to more than anything in the world," she said. "But I can't make any promises right now. We'll have to take things day by day."

He let out his breath in a frustrated hiss. "I think you've just earned yourself another spanking," he said.

CHAPTER THIRTEEN

The setting sun lit the horizon on fire, painting the tips of distant treetops red and yellow. Marigold stood in the backyard staring into the distance, arms folded, a frown creasing her face.

"That's not how you're supposed to look when you're standing out here in God's country,watching a beautiful sunset," Ginger said.

"I told Henry I couldn't see him anymore." Marigold's face was a mask of misery. Her eyes glittered with angry tears.

"Oh," Ginger said. "Was he bad in bed?"

"No, he was incredible. Ten out of ten. Wait, make that twenty out of ten."

"Was he rude while you were out on dates? Flirted with other women?"

"No, he held the door open for me, acted like I was the only woman in the world, and seemed fascinated with everything that I said."

"Wow. He sounds like such a douchebag. I'd have dumped him too."

"I know, right? What a dick." Marigold sounded aggrieved.

"Remind me again why we're mad at him?"

"Because he's acting like the perfect guy and then he's going to do whatever it is that he does that breaks my heart."

"Right. Of course. Dick." Ginger turned to walk back to the house, but then she stopped.

Just because her relationship was doomed didn't mean that everybody else's relationship had to be doomed. She tried to think about how to diplomatically approach the situation. How to get Marigold to see how foolish she was being.

"Marigold, you're being a total, pig-headed dumbass."

Oops. That hadn't come out in the loving, supportive manner that she'd meant it to. Maybe she was a teensy bit crabby because she was still stressed out about the situation with the sheriff.

"What?" Marigold said, shocked.

"Listen. Did it ever occur to you that you can affect the outcome of your psychic visions?"

Marigold started to protest, but Ginger held up her hand. "Hear me out. You're so burnt out and bitter from having lived through your mother's world-record-breaking number of divorces that you go into every relationship expecting it to fail. What if you decided to try your hardest to make this work?"

"Well, I-"

"I happened to have asked Loch about Henry. He said that word among the shifters is, Henry's talking non-stop about how much he likes you."

"Really?" Marigold blinked back tears. "But I already broke up with him. And he was really upset. It's probably too late."

"He was upset because he really likes you, you moron! Call him back and be honest with him. Tell him that you really really like him too, but you've been through so many bad relationships that it's hard for you to trust anybody."

"I saw myself in the future, going back to New York, alone!"

"But that's what happens if you have the mindset that no relationship is going to work. Look, happy relationships are out there. We've both seen them. My parents are a perfect example. Change your mindset, for God's sake. Go apologize to him now. Do something crazy, show up wearing lingerie under a coat or something like that."

"I – I -"

"Go! My love life may be screwed because apparently I'm the wrong color of wolf, but that doesn't mean that everybody else has to suffer."

"Well, if I'm a dumbass, so are you. You're giving up way too easily," Marigold said, and marched back to the farmhouse, leaving Ginger standing by herself watching the sun sink lower and lower into the horizon.

A sudden noise coming from behind the outhouse made Ginger start. She couldn't quite figure out what it was; it sounded like two raccoons fighting, but the scent from behind the outhouse was definitely human.

Carefully she crept behind the outhouse, peeking behind bushes to see…Winifred and the handyman, buck naked, on the ground. Their clothes lay in a pile next to them. Winifred was on top, straddling the handyman, head thrown back in ecstasy, riding him like a cowboy on a bucking bronco. Her hair flowed down her back and over her small breasts like a golden waterfall.

"Harder!" the handyman yelled. "Ride me like a bull!"

Good lord, she thought, even Winifred's got a better love life than me.

With a sinking heart, she turned and walked back to the boarding house. The wedding march ring tone sounded, and she reluctantly answered her phone. More bad news?

"You are not coming back to New York," her mother said. "You are going to stay there and marry that sheriff, and that's final."

"Hello. By the way, that's how normal people start their

phone conversations. They say hello. Maybe exchange a few pleasantries. How's the weather in New York?"

"Cloudy, with a chance of weddings. Listen. I spoke to your father. We are not going to allow Reynaldo Cruz bully us like that. He hasn't even given your father a raise in years. Your father is already updating his resume and putting out feelers with other firms."

"If the Alpha fires him and puts out the word not to hire him…"

"We could relocate to another pack, if we had to. This wedding is happening, damn it!"

"Mother, why are you so insanely determined to see me married?"

"Because meeting your father was the best thing that ever happened to me, and I have been ridiculously happy every day that I am married to him. Even when he annoys the living crap out of me, which is fairly frequently. I want that for you. The happy part, not the annoying part, but I think they go hand in hand, unfortunately."

"Oh." Sudden tears sprang to Ginger's eyes. It was true. Her parents were a living testament to the power of love. She yearned for what they had. "I could swear you just used a cuss word. You'd wash my mouth out with soap if I said that!"

"Well, I'm frustrated. This is ridiculous! Some jealous cow is trying to ruin your relationship because you and the sheriff are different types of wolf? I'm a witch and your father is a shifter. We couldn't possibly come from more different backgrounds , and we've been ridiculously happy for 30 years. And we have four of the most beautiful daughters any family could hope for. And I want some damn grandchildren to spoil while I'm still young enough to bend over and pick them up!"

"Good gracious, mother. Language. Watch your language. You really think that you and dad will be all right if I stay here?"

Her mother had already mentally moved on to more

important matters. "I'm trying to decide what type of paper you should choose for the wedding invitations. Also, there's a lot of different styles of calligraphy to consider and I think-"

"I am officially hanging up on you now. I love you, and you're insane. Seek professional help." Ginger clicked the "off" button, but as she walked up the back stairs, she allowed a little flutter of hope to quiver inside her heart.

Maybe she could stay here. Maybe she could keep Loch. Maybe her heart didn't have to break into a million pieces.

CHAPTER FOURTEEN

"So if you get married, can I be a bridesmaid?" Lola was leaning back in her chair with her combat boots propped up on the desk, flipping through the pages of a bridal magazine.

Ginger grabbed it away from her. "My God. You, my mother, Loch's grandmother…Why is everyone in the world so obsessed with marrying me off?"

Then she peered at the page Lola had been looking at. "That is a beautiful dress. Wow. Ivory silk. And look at those hand embroidered roses. You know- no, damn it! I will not be sucked into this madness! It is way too soon to be talking about weddings!" She threw the magazine back down on Lola's desk.

"Not around here. When the Alpha claims a mate, it's pretty much bam, boom, done. And an Alpha wedding is amazing. All the packs from all over the state come, and the party lasts for days. Think how many hot guys I'd meet." Lola pouted. "I'm bored with all the guys in Blue Moon. I need fresh flesh. Why can't you think about my needs?"

Ginger walked away, laughing. Then she glanced at the corner of the room and saw Jax glaring at his computer, lips pressed together in an angry line, and she sobered up a little.

She had a feeling that one way or another, Jax wasn't going to last with the sheriff's office much longer. He was a man of action, he had the temperament if not the self-restraint of an Alpha, and there was no way he'd put up with a desk job forever.

She looked up to see Loch walking out of his office, towards her.

"There's been a break in the case," he said.

"What break?"

"We got an anonymous tip from a disposable phone, telling us to search Tommy Deerkiller's house. And Montgomery actually agreed to let us come on to Panther Nation property so we could do the search;he agreed this case needs to be resolved. We found the professor's clothes hidden under Deerkiller's bed. They were shredded, as if by panther claws, and they're blood-staine.d We've been investigating Deerkiller for some time now, even before the professor's disappearance, for suspicion of dealing in stolen Panther Nation artifacts."

Loch didn't look happy as he said it, though.

"What is it?"

"I just don't like it." Loch shook his head. "I don't know why, because everything ties together neatly, and we do know for a fact that Tommy deals in stolen goods, but something doesn't smell right here."

"I agree, there's something off about it. Who made the anonymous call? Why would Tommy hide the professor's clothes at his house? And if he was the professor's inside man, why would he kill him?"

"Theoretically, they could have argued over money. The professor could have threatened to blackmail him." He sighed and shook his head. "Nothing we can do about it right now, anyway. Tommy's lawyered up. My grandmother's holding a barbecue at her place tomorrow afternoon, by the way. She invited you."

She held up her hand to argue with him, and he shook his head. "Ginger, let me worry about the pack. Just come, all right?"

"That's a very public statement you'd be making."

"Yes it is." He looked at her steadily, and she felt her heart swelling in her chest. He wanted her, and he wasn't afraid who knew it. He'd be proud to be seen by her side. The thought took her breath way.

Stil, when she went back to the boarding house that evening she felt strange and unsettled. She felt as if they were missing something important. And she knew damned well that the professor wasn't dead. Her powers had never steered her wrong before.

Tommy Deerkiller had, of course, vociferously denied knowing anything about the bloody clothes in his room. He'd denied killing the professor, communicating with the professor about selling him icons, or seeing him on the night the professor disappeared.

But he admitted that he'd been dealing in stolen property.

Odd, Ginger thought.

When Ginger walked in the door, Marigold was waiting for her.

She told her that three of the archeology students had gone home already. There was no point in staying; it was pretty obvious that the professor wasn't coming back. "Also, heads up, Brenda and Tallulah are in a snit because you told them the professor was alive and now the bloody clothes make it look like he's dead."

Brenda and Tallulah, their rivalry apparently forgotten, were sitting on the living room couch crying on each others' shoulders.

They both looked up and glared at her when she came in.

"Fraud," Brenda hissed, her eyes swollen into little slits from crying.

"You got our hopes up for no reason," Tallulah sniffled self-righteously.

Ginger tried to speak, but they both got up and flounced out of the room.

"Damn it," Ginger said unhappily. "I know that I'm right. He's not dead."

"I have news that might cheer you up," Marigold said. "Not professor-related news, but still…"

Ginger peered at her closely. "Oh my God, you've got that I've-just-had-multiple orgasms look about you. Henry forgave you and you had makeup sex. In the middle of the day. Only a complete floozy does that. I know from personal experience."

"It's even better than that." Marigold was glowing with satisfaction.

"Better? What's better than you and Henry and makeup sex?"

"Winifred and the handyman. Sittin' in a tree."

"Okay, explain this to me, without the use of nursery rhymes. I could desperately use some good news."

"Yesterday Winifred came to ask me if there was any hope for her and the handyman. I looked in her future and saw Winifred crying in her room and the handyman driving off in frustration."

"Okay. And this is good news because?"

"I was about to tell her that, but then I thought about what you told me. Winifred was asking me for a reading, in her own barely comprehensible geek speak, because she was afraid that it wouldn't work out. She was afraid that they were too different. And you were the one who told me that when you expect the end of a relationship, you end up unconsciously sabotaging yourself."

"True."

"So I asked her if she wanted it to work out with him, and she said yes. I asked her what she saw as the potential barriers to it working out, and she told me. Then I told her to pretend she was writing a thesis on why it could work out, and to come up with solutions to all of the problems that she found."

"And?"

"And then I looked into my crystal ball again and I saw them, I am not kidding you, with wedding rings, and each of them holding a twin baby in their arms. And I told her it would work out. And this morning she told me that apparently you don't have to connect intellectually with a person to be happy, as long as you connect emotionally. Well, she said it much geekier, but that was pretty much the gist."

Her smile grew mischievous. "And she had bite marks on her neck this morning. And her shirt was buttoned up wrong."

Ginger gasped. Winifred was an obsessive neat freak. "It must be love!"

"I know, right?" Then her face fell. "But Ginger, if I can affect the outcomes of my readings, than I've ruined relationships for no reasons. I've broken up people who might have gotten married! Oh, my God-"

Ginger quickly made a shushing motion. "Don't do that to yourself, Marigold. There's no guarantee that you could have talked those people into trying to work things out. Most of them probably would still have probably gone on to ruin things for themselves, and you know what? People can survive a breakup. The question is, what are you going to do with your new found powers, now that you've found a new approach to your love readings?"

"Well, Henry would like me to stay here and give things between us a try. And Winifred told Imogen about how well things worked out with my reading, and Imogen spread the word, so I'm getting a lot of requests."

"Would you miss New York?"

"Sure. But it's not like a prison sentence. I can visit. And there's things that I like about it here, too."

Marigold looked at Ginger through narrowed eyes. "And you're staying, right? Because you're not a complete fool?"

"It's not that simple," Ginger said.

"This is ridiculous," Marigold grumbled. "What does that bitch of a council member think that she'd get if she broke up you and Sheriff Hot Stuff? It's not like he's suddenly going to turn around and marry Portia."

"Maybe she's fooled herself into thinking that might happen. Or maybe it's just spite; if Portia can't have him, she doesn't want anyone to have him."

"Maybe."

The next day…

At 11 a.m., Ginger glided to a stop on the street in front of Willie's house and parked Imogen's pickup truck behind a patrol car. There were dozens of cars there already.

Everyone had congregated behind the house. As she strolled up, she could hear country music blaring from a boombox, and a happy babble of voices. There were easily a hundred people there.

As she walked up to a table laden with plates of corn on the cob and biscuits and bowls of fruit, she was surprised to see Cletus and his younger brothers and sisters there, sitting cross-legged on the grass hunched over their paper plates. Their faces were smeared with barbecue sauce and there were piles of gnawed bones on the plates.

He looked up at her and flashed her a big grin. "The sheriff invited me," he said. "That was real nice of him. I guess he's not all bad."

"Not all bad," she agreed. "He has his good points. Wipe your faces, kids." She winced when Cletus obligingly wiped his face on his sleeve and his younger siblings followed suit, but she decided to give it a pass. He'd done what she told him to, hadn't she?

She headed over to Lola, who was standing with her arm around a Goth-looking Coyote shifter.

"Hey, Ginger. Beer?" Lola said, holding up a bottle of Corona with ice chips clinging to it.

"Give me that." Ginger grabbed it from her hands as a group of wolf shifters headed straight for her. "I'm going to need it. And more. Are they all going to interrogate me?"

"But of course. His parents will be here soon."

"What?" It came out in a squeak. She downed half the bottle in one gulp.

"Remember. Bridesmaid. And don't be picking any butt ugly bridesmaid's dresses, either. I don't look good in yellow. Washes me out."

"The world has gone mad. You must have something better to do than planning my non-existent wedding for me."

"Not really, which is actually kind of sad when you think of it," Lola said cheerfully.

The wolf shifters crowded around Ginger, peppering her with questions.

"Are you moving in with him right away, or are you going to live somewhere in town?" A heavy-set woman with a bouffant asked her.

"Are you going to marry my uncle?" a little boy said, yanking on her skirt.

"Can I be your flower girl?" a little blonde girl piped up. "I like flowers. Will you pick me some flowers?"

"Oh, my goodness. Look, is that Dora the Explorer standing over there?"

When they turned to look, she turned and ran.

Suddenly she was grabbed from behind, by two strong muscular arms. She didn't need to turn around; his familiar scent sent a wave of delicious heat sizzling through her.

Smiling, she spun into his arms.

"That was a dirty trick," he grinned.

"It was a matter of survival. It was them or me. I had to escape."

With a huge smile, he added, "How's this for a dirty

trick?" And then he said very loudly, "Ginger Colby, will you dance with me? Please?"

Everyone turned and stared. Everyone held their breath.

Ginger Colby was no fool. She wasn't going to make the same mistake twice.

She made a big show of doing a graceful half curtsy and answered loudly "Of course, I will dance with you."

He swept her into his arms as Wilhelmina turned up the boom-box, and the two of them spun around on the grass. Ginger loved to dance, but Ashmont had always acted as if he were afraid she'd fall on him and break him.

But Loch spun and twirled Ginger as if she were light as a feather. He dipped her backwards until her hair brushed the grassy lawn. He spun her like a top.

And when the music stopped, the crowd burst into applause.

"Ginger Colby, there's something else that I want to ask you," the sheriff said loudly. Ginger froze.

Seriously? Was he going to ask her what she thought he was going to ask her?

And how would she respond?

"No, you don't." A shrill voice cracked across the lawn.

Ginger turned, her heart sinking in her chest. Portia Sinclair and an elegantly dressed woman who looked like an older version of Portia were walking across the lawn towards them. Portia wore jeans, strappy high heeled sandals, and a clingy, silky t-shirt, and her lip curled in disgust when her eyes lighted on Ginger. The woman wore a tailored linen suit that fit her narrow frame like a glove, and she carefully picked her away across the grass in high heeled pumps.

There were two Werewolf Enforcers with them, in uniform, tall muscular men with buzz cuts and grim, expressions stamped on their faces. The Enforcers worked for the council.

"Aurora Sinclair, you were not invited. Get off my property," Willie snapped, eyes blazing with anger.

"I'm sorry, Willhelmina, but this is council business." Aurora turned to Loch, who looked as if he were about to explode with anger.

"She is a red wolf. You are a gray." Aurora spoke in clipped tones. "If you two mate, your pups will not be pure. For the good of the council, if you insist on continuing this relationship, I will be forced to order your removal as Alpha and replace you with Jax."

Ginger gasped in horror. Hot-headed Jax? That would be an utter disaster. He would have the Blue Moon wolves at war with the panther nation before the week was out. Every wolf shifter in Blue Moon County would be in danger.

Her parents, Loch's pack…she couldn't do this. She just couldn't. There were too many good people that she'd hurt if she selfishly insisted on staying. There was much more at stake here than her own happiness.

As Loch started to protest, Ginger spoke up, eyes filling with hot tears.

"Stop!" she shouted. "I'm going back to New York, tonight. It's over, Loch. That's my choice."

She turned and ran back to her car.

Behind her she heard howls of rage, and snarls. It sounded as if Loch was clashing violently with the Enforcers. She knew he'd be all right, because he had dozens of his relatives there.

But she had to get out of there right away, she knew, before she changed her mind.

She drove down the road blindly, tears streaming down her face, her heart aching. She'd been so close to happiness.

Loch was right, he was her fated mate. Every time he came near her, her heart sang. How could this be? How could she find her fated mate and be torn away from him? Why was fate such a cruel bitch?

Crying so hard she had to gulp out her words between

sobs, she called Marigold to tell her what happened, and asked Marigold to pack her bags and meet her in an hour at a gas station on the edge of town. She couldn't bear to set foot in the boarding house again, couldn't bear to face Loch if he came to the boarding house and tried to change her mind.

CHAPTER FIFTEEN

She turned off her cell phone and drove aimlessly, down country roads she'd never see again. She rolled down the windows so she could feel the breeze caress her face and hear the birds sing one last time.

When she showed up at the gas station, she was shocked to see that Marigold and Brenda were both waiting for her, and Brenda looked frantic.

"I found this under my door," she said, and thrust a note at Ginger.

"Jax and a gang of wolves started a fight with the panthers, and a bunch of them are at the hospital now," Marigold said at the same time. "And the panthers grabbed Jax and kidnapped him."

"What?" Ginger's jaw dropped. "Slow down. What the hell is going on?"

She looked at the note. "The professor told me not to tell anyone, but I had to let you know so you wouldn't be sad any more. He's not dead. He asked me to come with him and be his bride. Don't worry, Brenda, you'll find your own true love some day. I'll tell you more when I can." It was signed, Tallulah.

Ginger felt an icy chill radiating from the note, and her heart dropped to the bottom of her shoes. She closed her eyes and concentrated, opening her mind.

Tallulah was dead, and she had died violently. She could sense it.

She blinked hard, tears burning her eyes. She didn't want to tell Brenda and Marigold until she was absolutely sure, but deep in her heart she knew.

"What happened with Jax?" she asked in a shaky voice.

"We drove to the sheriff's station with this note and gave it to Jax," Marigold said. "He said he'd take care of it himself, because the sheriff never does anything. I guess he rounded up some wolves and they went to the Panther Nation and tried to muscle their way in, and it started a huge fight. The wolves were injured, and they ran off, and Jax was dragged away by the panthers."

Ginger's heart sank.

She didn't dare go talk to Loch. She might weaken. Or Aurora might see her talking to him, and take away Loch's position as Alpha on the spot.

"I'll go try to talk to Montgomery," she said. "We've got to find out what happened to Tallulah. And if the professor's still alive, maybe he's hiding out on panther territory still. Maybe he had help. If Montgomery actually let people on to his territory to arrest Tommy Deerkiller, I think he's coming around and he'll listen to reason."

"I feel like something really bad's happened to her," Brenda said. "Has it?"

"I'm not sure yet," Ginger lied.

"I feel terrible for all those times that I said mean things to her."

"You were both victims of the professor. He's been alive all this time and letting both of you suffer? He manipulated you both. He played you against each other."

"I see that now." Brenda nodded, and tears filled her eyes.

She put her hand on Ginger's arm. "Be careful, Ginger. I'm sorry I've been such a naggy, annoying pain in the ass."

"You weren't at all," Ginger assured her.

Yes you were, Ginger thought.

With her heart aching for poor Tallulah, Ginger quickly headed out to panther territory. Her head was in a whirl; what the hell was going on here? What would she find there?

When she arrived at the gates that led into their territory, she identified herself to the shifter in the guard shack.

He spoke to someone on the radio, and then came back and nodded to Ginger.

"Wait here," he said to her.

A few minutes later a car pulled up, and the panther in the car gestured to her to follow him. With shaking hands, she followed him down a narrow country road.

There were no telephone poles out here, no electric poles. The trees loomed like ancient giants, dark and swaying in the wind, and she had an uneasy feeling churning in her stomach as they reached a sprawling wooden structure that was more like a compound than a house.

She parked and climbed out, and with every step she took she felt more and more certain that she'd made a terrible mistake coming out here by herself.

She paused at the front door, hesitating. Should she just turn around and leave?

Before she had a chance to decide, Montgomery opened the door. "I'm glad to see you," he said, grim-faced. "We've got a problem, and I don't know what to do about it. I need to talk to you."

"Is Jax here?" she asked him anxiously.

"He's here. I'll let you talk to him in just a minute."

She swallowed hard, her palms damp with perspiration. If Jax was there, she had to go in. He was probably injured. She might be able to sweet talk Montgomery into letting her take Jax with her.

She followed him into the house. Hand woven rugs in geometric patterns adorned the floor. The walls were plaster, and paintings of panther shifters decorated the walls without frames.

Something felt very wrong here. Somebody was trying to speak to her from the other side, pounding at the edges of her consciousness. Tallulah? She wondered. But how would Tallulah have reached her here? She needed to be touching something that had belonged to the dead, or in their home or a place they'd spent a lot of time, before she could communicate with them.

Jason Strikes True and Richard Iron Claw were standing in the spacious living room, still as statues, with their arms by their sides. They had odd expressions on their faces. A ripple of alarm ran down Ginger's spine as she noticed that the curtains were all drawn. It made the house feel like a dim, closed-in prison.

"Hello, Jason. How are you?" she said.

He stared at her, his eyes bulging, and his lip quivered, but he didn't speak.

Suddenly Montgomery's radio crackled.

"Sheriff Armstrong is at the gate. He's asking to speak to you," a voice said.

"Perfect. Send him back here," Montgomery said.

Perfect? Ginger thought with alarm.

What did he mean by that? Why was it perfect?

"Come with me," Montgomery said. He nodded at Jason and Richard. "You come too," he said.

Well, at least Loch would be there, she thought with growing unease. She followed Montgomery down a long hallway, with Jason and Richard right behind her.

Montgomery led her through several doors and into a large library with books stacked high on the walls, and as she walked through the doorway, the coppery tang of blood filled her nostrils.

She froze on the spot and spun around, but before she could run, Montgomery nodded his head at Jason and Richard. "Grab her," he said. "Bring her in the room."

They both leaped forward and grabbed her by the arms, dragging her across the floor. She struggled and screamed, but it was useless. Their grip was like iron

The smell of blood was overpowering. Glancing at the back of the room, she saw where it was coming from. A body lay on a wooden table, wrapped in a tarp. Flies buzzed around it. There was a bloodstained knife resting on top of the body, with a cruel curved blade.

It was Tallulah. She could sense it.

Ginger wanted to scream, or cry, but the sound died in her throat.

She suddenly realized with shock that Jax was sitting in a chair by the table, his arms by his side. He was staring straight ahead with a blank expression on his face. His lip was split, one of his eyes was blacked, and the right side of his face was swollen.

"Jax!" Ginger cried out. "What are you doing? Help me!"

He blinked hard but didn't move.

"I'm afraid he's not capable, my dear," the professor's voice said. "I own his mind now. I own his will. And soon I will own yours."

Montgomery walked around to stand in front of her. His face began to melt. The professor's wavy hair appeared, his face...

Professor Reese stood before her. He had several small stone icons dangling from a leather cord on his neck.

"Where is Montgomery?" she gasped. "Did you kill him?"

"Oh, of course. The night I disappeared."

Yes. That was who had been hammering at her mind, trying to get her to open up. Montgomery. As soon as she'd walked in he'd tried to warn her.

She heard Loch walking down the hall and she struggled

to scream, to warn him. "Cover her mouth," the professor said to Richard, and Richard clamped his hand firmly over her mouth, pinning her in place. Ginger writhed and bit at Richard's hand until it bled, but he didn't move.

Should she shift? There wasn't much point; she was in a room with two panther shifters who could easily take her wolf down.

Loch entered the room a minute later, and froze for a second in shock when he saw the scene before him, with Ginger restrained and struggling. Then he let out a roar of rage and lunged forward.

Professor Reese waved the stone icon and said a few words, and Loch went crashing down to his knees, and his eyes glazed over.

"Stand up," Professor Reese barked. Loch stood up. "Sit at the table, in that chair," Reese ordered, and the sheriff did as he was told.

"What did you do to him?" Ginger gasped.

"You're next, you know," Professor Reese smiled gently, the way he did when he was asking one of his students to fetch him coffee. "You'll still be able to understand what's going on around you, and feel rage and despair and humiliation. But you won't be able to do a damned thing about it. I could tell you to gauge your own eyes out, and you'd do it."

Ginger's heart was pounding so hard she thought it would crack through her rib cage.

Was Loch's mind gone forever? Was there no saving him? The thought made her so angry that her vision swam red. Her mate. Loch was her mate. Professor Reese was hurting her mate.

She needed to stall. This couldn't be the end. Ginger Colby was not a quitter. "Tell me what happened first," she pleaded.

His smile spread wider. He was a raging egomaniac, and she knew he couldn't resist the urge to brag.

He turned to Jason. "Tell them what you did," he ordered him. "Tell him about how you brought about the end of the Panther nation."

A tear glittered in Jason's eye, and he blinked hard, and began talking, in a wooden, despairing voice.

"I was supposed to guard the icons," he said. "It was my sacred duty, but I let myself be distracted by Tommy Deerkiller's daughter. While we were in the woods together, someone broke in to the hut where we keep them. It was probably Tommy; we've known for a long time that he was stealing and selling sacred panther items. I heard the noise and ran back there and interrupted the burglary, but it was too late. Someone had disturbed the wooden box which held the most powerful of icons, the Mind-stealer. The box was on the floor and there were stone amulets scattered all over. I told my father. He said that it was high time we found a way to destroy the icon, but we didn't know which one it was."

"How could you not know?"

He stayed silent.

"Answer her," Reese said.

"We never open the box. We simply guard it. It hasn't been opened in centuries, since the death of River Runs Red. We thought that there was only the Mind-stealer in there. We were shocked to see all the icons scattered on the floor."

Ginger glanced over at Loch. His face twitched, his eyes blazing with anger, but he stayed frozen where he sat.

"Richard and his father contacted me at the university, and secretly hired me to come out here and look through the icons and identify the Mind-stealer," Professor Reese said with a smile. "I set up the dig so that I could get close to the panther's property, and then Richard and Jason arranged for a disturbance on the far edge of the property to distract everyone, so I could have time to come on the property and look at the icons in the hut where they're guarded. I saw the shape-shifter icon in there, recognized it, and changed shape just as Montgomery came into the hut to confront me."

"You killed him and took his place," Ginger said. "Why take his place?"

"For all kinds of reasons. For power. For fun. To hide the fact that I'd killed him. So I could stay on the property and look through all of the icons at my leisure. I'm the ruler of the panther nation now. I've been fucking every young panther woman I fancy. It's been delightful." He grinned, and his eyes had a mad glow to them. Jason's face twitched with anger, but he stood still as a statue.

"Jason's sister was particularly tight and delicious. I fucked her in every hole," The professor taunted. "Of course, she cried when I popped her cherry, and she cried even harder when I took her up the ass, but no panther dares to refuse the orders of Montgomery Eagle Feather. She could barely walk when I finished using her. Limped out of her bleeding, and wailing like a kitten."

Jason's lips quivered.

"Got something to say, Jason?" the professor grinned.

Jason stood silently, with murder blazing in his eyes.

"Why did you kill Tallulah?" Ginger blinked back tears.

"Ahh, yes. Quite sad. Tallulah was an angel, wasn't she? But it had to be done, you see. The Mind Stealer is the most powerful icon of all, giving the wearing complete control over any shifter…but it is only activated by the fresh blood of a human virgin."

Ginger felt as if she were going to vomit. Tallulah must have been overjoyed when she saw the professor again, and over the moon when he asked her to marry him. She'd eagerly run off to her death. Ginger could only pray it had been quick.

"When did you kill her?"

"Last night. The people here were starting to suspect me.

Jason and Richard came to confront me. I needed to gain control of them."

"If the icon gets its power from fresh blood, won't the power wear off?" she asked despairingly.

"Yes, it will. I will have to re-activate it at every full moon, with a fresh human virgin. That won't be a problem. Killing is surprisingly easy after the first time."

"It doesn't work perfectly. These people here are still fighting you. If anyone saw them out in public, they'd know something was wrong."

"It takes time. The longer I have people under my control, the weaker their minds become. I'm still experimenting, learning my way around these icons. But the day will come when I control all of the shifter leaders in the nation. And now…it's your turn."

He pointed the stone icon at Ginger and said the words again. She froze in place.

"Let go of her," he said to Richard. Richard released her arm.

He pointed at the table. "Go sit down," he told her. She walked over to the table and sat down, staring at Tallulah's body. The smell of blood was overwhelming, threatening to choke her.

How long had it taken Tallulah to die? She wondered, blinking back tears. What had her final thoughts been?

He walked up behind her, and ran his fingers through her hair.

"I'm going to make you watch while I fuck your fated mate," he told Loch. "She's going to suck me dry. She's going to howl like a dog for me. Then I think I'll have her fuck every panther shifter under my control, all at the same time. We'll have a big, delightful orgy. I might even make you join in."

Ginger felt fear and nausea swirling inside her. She was so terrified that she was light-headed, her heart pounding in her chest. She could feel her lunch roiling in her stomach and struggled not to vomit on the table in front of her.

Loch quivered, but couldn't move.

"Isn't this fun, Ginger?" Professor Reese grinned, bent down, and ran his tongue up her neck. She sat frozen in place.

The professor turned and started to walk away.

Ginger's hand shot out. She grabbed the blood-stained knife that lay next to Tallulah's body, and leaped through the air, knocking the professor to the ground. He hit the floor with a surprised oof.

Big girl power, she thought.

Before he could move or bark a command to his enslaved thralls, she'd slashed the leather cord holding the stone icons, and yanked it from his neck. The icons scattered and bounced on the wooden floor.

"What? How?" His eyes were wild with fright and shock.

Her fangs sprang out, and her eyes blazed with rage. "I'm only half shifter," she snarled. "So the spell didn't work on me. Stay down, or I'll kill you."

Something black appeared in her peripheral vision, and the next thing she knew, two huge panthers who had been Jason and Richard knocked her away and sent her rolling on the ground. And then Loch and Jax joined them, in wolf form, huge and gray and howling with fury.

She heard roars, and claws rending flesh, and horrible, horrible screams that grew higher and higher in pitch. She covered her face with her hands; there was nothing that she could do to stop the enraged shifters.

The screaming turned to wet gurgling.

She felt strong hands on her. Loch was in human form again, kneeling next to her.

Loch pulled her to feet and she collapsed into his arms, weeping, her knees trembling so hard she could barely stand.

CHAPTER SIXTEEN

"Are you sure you're okay?" Loch asked for the millionth time.

"Fine. I'm fine." Ginger's voice was steady but her hands were still shaking.

She was sitting in the sheriff's office with Winifred, Loch, Lola and Marigold crowded around her. Lola had bought her an ice pack which she pressed against her temples; she had a throbbing headache from the whole ordeal.

"I just heard from Marcus Running Horse, who was the Panther Nation's second in command. He's temporary leader while they convene and figure out what to do next," Loch said. "This is unprecedented."

"What about the icons?"

"They're going to modernize their security. Build a massive vault to store the icons in."

"What about Tommy Deerkiller?"

"He's still going to be prosecuted for dealing in stolen property. He'll likely get a few years in prison. Obviously he didn't kill anyone. It appears that the professor, disguised as Montgomery is the one who framed him, put the bloody clothes in his house and called us from a disposable phone to tip us off."

Ginger nodded, wearily. "I still can't believe Tallulah's dead. That poor, silly, naïve girl. Have you notified her parents?"

"Yes." Loch's face was resigned and sad. "The part of my job that I hate the most. They're flying in to claim the body."

"At least this hideous ordeal is over with," Marigold said.

"Most of it. We've still got the Wolf Shifter Council gunning for us," Ginger pointed out.

"No, you don't. You didn't stick around at the barbecue to see what happened," Willie said. "I told Aurora that I'm planning on making an immediate challenge for her council seat. You should have seen her face. She went white as a sheet."

"You can do that?"

"Yes. It requires 90 percent of the vote to pass, and normally it's just about impossible to unseat a council member, but Aurora's very, very unpopular, and she knows it. Her family's been throwing their weight around for years. And everyone knows that she tried to replace Loch with Jax. After what Jax pulled, openly attacking the panthers and nearly starting a war, that makes her look like a fool. She's going to lose her council seat, big time."

"I can stay?" Ginger's eyes lit up, and suddenly she felt as if she could breathe again.

"I was never going to let you go," Loch's voice came out in a growl.

He went down on one knee and took her hand in his.

"You're going to ask me to marry you, right here and now?" Ginger asked.

"No, not now. What I am going to do is, I'm going to tell you that I'm going to ask you to marry me, when a little time has passed, when we've put this day behind us. I love you. When you're not with me, I ache for you. You are my fated mate, and you are here where you belong."

"Oh." Ginger's voice was husky with emotion. "Well,

when you ask me to marry you, I will say yes. Because now that I've met you, I believe in fated mates. I never did before, and I fought it every step of the way, but I can't fight it any more. I love you so much it hurts. You are the one for me. And I will dance with you any time that you ask."

EPILOGUE

"You're sure that you want to do this?" Loch said, as they pulled up in front of the battered metal shell that served as the Arbuckle residence.

"Rather than have Cletus' family taken away and placed with strangers? Yes," Ginger said firmly. "You know what that would do to him. He'd fight you like crazy, and it would be horribly traumatic for everyone, and then he'd probably quit work and fall to pieces. I think he'd be okay with me stepping in as foster parent until he turns 18. He likes me. I'm the best alternative."

She'd stalled Loch as long as she could, but Loch had finally put his foot down. He had to uphold the law. He couldn't leave four young children living in a house with only a minor to supervise them, and Cletus was still a minor.

"It's too bad," Loch said, shaking his head. "The house looks the best I've seen it in years. He's obviously doing a pretty good job keeping it up."

The house actually did look as if someone was taking the best possible care of it. The lawn was mowed, there were fresh geraniums planted out front in a bed of mulch, and someone had washed the metal exterior recently and slapped a fresh coat of paint on the shutters.

The door swung open, and Cletus walked out. When he saw Ginger and Loch, his face lit up in a smile, to Ginger's surprise.

"You heard about my ma?" he asked.

A woman appeared behind him, and walked down the steps, holding a broom in one hand, which she set down on the stairs. She was older, with a weary, lined face and brown hair shot through with gray and pulled back in a bun. She wore a faded dress and had holes in her dirty sneakers.

"You're back?" Loch's jaw dropped.

"I went away to rehab. I haven't had a drink in a month now," she said proudly.

Loch peered at her. "By god, you're right. If you had I could scent it on you. You should have told someone where you were going, though. You should have arranged for care for your kids."

She looked down at the ground, ashamed. "I know I should have. I was just so afraid I'd screw up, and let everyone down again. But I'm back now for good. That man at the community center, where Cletus works, he gave me a job cleaning up." She smiled proudly. "He said Cletus is a real hard worker. Best one he's got. He said any family of Cletus, he'd be proud to have on his payroll."

Loch nodded slowly. "See that you stay clean this time, Emmaline. You pretty much are out of second chances."

She bobbed her head earnestly. "I know. I know."

Ginger pulled Cletus aside. "That was your wish, wasn't it? At the wishing well? You wished for your mother to come back?" she said in a low voice.

He nodded, his eyes suddenly glittering with tears that he blinked away quickly.

"It worked, didn't it?" he said proudly.

"It most certainly did. Because we're in Blue Moon County, where wishes come true."

***

What's next? The Bobcat's Tale, curvy bobcat shifter Lainey Robinson and Alpha deputy Tate's story!

Don't miss out on future sales and new releases! Subscribe to my newsletter here! I shifty swear to never spam you or share your information!

BOOKS BY GEORGETTE ST. CLAIR

The Alpha Billion-weres Series

The Billion-were Needs a Mate

A Cub for the Billion-were

The Billion-Were Claims His Mate

Timber Valley Pack Series

Bride of the Alpha

Purr for the Alpha

Hard as Steele

Lynx on the Loose

Taken by the Alpha

The Alpha Won't be Denied

Blue Moon Junction Series

The Alpha claims a Mate

The Bobcat's Tale

Hard to Bear

My Heart Laid Bear

Shifters, Inc.

The Alpha Meets His Match

His Purrfect Mate

Pixie the Lion Tamer

The Bear Who Loved Me

Spotting His Leopard

Blackmailed by the Wolf

The Mating Game Series

Big Bad Wolf

A Grizzly Kind of Love

Starcrossed Dating Agency Series

The Vulfan's True Mate

The Dragon Claims His Treasure

The Vulfan's Dark Desires

Bridenapped Series

The Alpha Chronicles

The Alpha's Choice

Tri-Valley Dragon Series

Bride of the Dragon

Dating a Dragon

Love Burns

Twin Alphas Series

Claimed

Desired

Alpha Prime Series

Shiftily Ever After

His Curvy Mate

Portal City Protectors

Mated to the Capo

Mated to the Enforcer

Mated to the Prince

Fated to the Traitor

Mated to the Chaos

Mated to the Moon

Standalone

Furrever Yours

The Dragon's Christmas Wish

Hello, I am Georgette St. Clair, writer of hot, sexy romances which star all Alpha heroes, all the time. The road to love may be rocky and fraught with peril, (and humor and scorchtastic sex and healthy heapings of snark) but my shifters will stop at nothing to claim their fated mate.

A little about me: I live in Florida. My checkered career involved stints as a newspaper reporter, EMT, internet marketer, cocktail waitress, temp, nurse's aide (but not all at the same time...)

Now I'm living my perfect life, spending my days in a fantasy universe where I nudge my smart-mouthed, take-no-guff heroines onto the path that will set them on a collision course with true love.

Check out my website for a complete list of titles and what's coming soon. Or connect with me on Facebook.